DRAG

PRELUDES & OMENS

MATT,

STEP THROUGH

THIS GATE!

DRAGONSGATE
PRELUDES & OMENS

James Maxey

Cover art by Keven Spain
Internal art by James Maxey

The author may be contacted at
james@jamesmaxey.net

ISBN-13: 978-1727160628

ISBN-10: 1727160622

For anyone hunted, haunted, or hurt.

HUNTED

HUNTED

GRAXEN CROUCHED on a sturdy branch in a tall oak at the edge of the forest, watching the meadow beyond. It was late evening, in the heart of summer. The meadow was alive with birds and bees, with verdant grass and blackberry vines giving the air sweetness, but the life that had caught Graxen's eyes was the stag. The stag one of the largest he'd seen, far too large for him to carry much more than a hindquarter back with him, and he was already regretting all he'd leave behind for the buzzards. The meat they'd smoked and dried from Nadala's last deer would be gone in a day or two, even though Graxen ate only a fraction of his share. Without a fresh kill, the grim prospect of starvation loomed.

The stag looked around cautiously as it chewed. Graxen sat motionless, feeling the breeze lightly teasing his feather-scales. The stag was upwind, unable to smell Graxen, and almost perfectly due south across the field, so that his shadow wouldn't cross the stag's path as he approached. The one potential obstacle was noise. Graxen could glide silently, but the deer was a quarter mile away, much too far to cover the full distance without flapping his wings. With a twenty foot wingspan, a single beat of his wings would be enough to alert the stag.

Graxen shifted Nadala's spear from his fore-talon to a hind-talon, still weighing his options. It would take no more than fifteen or twenty seconds to cross the field. He could launch with a beat of his wings, gain altitude, and glide the full distance, hoping the noise of his initial wingbeat didn't reach the buck. Or, he could spread his wings silently and glide half the distance, then beat his wings for a burst of speed, alerting the deer. At full speed, he could cover the remaining ground in seconds. The stag was no more than a hundred feet from the opposite tree line. Could the buck reach the trees before Graxen overtook him?

The shadows were growing longer. In a few more minutes, the sun would vanish. The stag turned his back to Graxen, walking nearer to the tree line, ten, twenty, thirty feet, before lowering its head again to nibble a fresh patch of grass.

Graxen spread his wings and fell forward, grasping his hunting spear tightly with both hind-talons. The branch creaked as his weight lifted, his wings clipping twigs and leaves as he emerged from the canopy. Graxen didn't even breathe as he waited for the deer to react. No reaction came. Graxen advanced silently on the wind, dropping lower, lower, the distance closing, but not as swiftly as he hoped. The weight of the spear slowed him, causing him to drop at a steeper angle than he'd calculated, until he was low enough that the tip of the spear grazed one of the taller bushes. *Now!*

Graxen flapped with all his strength. The buck startled, its head lifting high. Graxen kept flapping, racing toward his target, still low to the ground. The buck leapt, reaching nearly the same height as Graxen as it bounded through the high brush. Graxen's heart beat rapidly as he realized he stood a chance, that he was closing on the deer faster than it was gaining on the forest.

Unfortunately, if he kept moving at the same speed, he'd be so close to the trees when he overtook the stag he was certain to crash. Injuring himself here, twenty miles distant from Nadala, could prove fatal to them both. He veered upward and hurled the spear. His aim was true... if the stag hadn't swerved suddenly to the left. The spear buried itself into the earth with a loud *THUNK* mere feet from the deer's hooves. The noise seemed to fill the beast with a supernatural power and it gave its farthest, fastest leap yet, seeming to fly into the shadows of the forest.

Graxen landed on a high branch, breathing heavily, listening to the crash and crunch of the stag in headlong flight through the forest, the noise growing fainter with each second as the stag gained distance. With a sigh, Graxen glided down to the meadow, landing beside the spear, which jutted from a thicket of blackberries. Thorns raked his sensitive fore-talons as he grasped the shaft. He pulled it free with a grunt. In the fading light, he studied the iron spear point. The tip was bent again. Hopefully it would survive being hammered back into shape once more.

As the last of the light faded, he rose into the air and headed back to the new cave he'd found. He vowed to rise before dawn and return to the meadow. The stag couldn't be the only deer that found the meadow attractive. When he returned tomorrow to lead Nadala here, he knew the prospect of fresh meat waiting for them both would buoy their spirits.

Unfortunately, a long day of exploration had left him exhausted beyond words. When he finally woke, the sun had been up for hours, and the deer were long gone from the meadow.

GRAXEN WAS WEARY, hot, and hungry. In flight, he could have covered the distance they'd slogged along the stony, steep mountainside in minutes. On foot, it had taken all day, and he estimated their progress to be only a few miles. Even those few miles travelled might have felt like progress, if only he had more confidence about where they were going.

Nadala followed close behind him, using the spear as a staff, treading carefully among the rocks and roots to keep her balance. Sky-dragons were ill-suited for hiking, but Nadala's pregnancy had advanced to a stage where flight was no longer an option. Her center of gravity had shifted, making her unsteady in the air, and her landings on her last few brief, tiresome flights had been less than graceful.

"We should rest," said Graxen, as he skittered down a steep slope to a large, flat rock. Beyond the edge of the rock, the mountainside dropped sharply, not quite a cliff, but a fall descending it would almost certainly lead to an unstoppable tumble all the way down to the rocky creek far below.

"We can't rest," said Nadala, sounding even more aggravated than the last five times he'd made the suggestion.

"You're going to hurt yourself, pushing too hard to keep walking when you're worn out," said Graxen.

"I'm a valkyrie," said Nadala. "I've trained to fight after days without food or water or even sleep."

"Did you train to fight when pregnant?" asked Graxen.

Nadala's eyes narrowed. "Obviously not."

"You don't need to prove to me how tough you are," said Graxen.

"Don't I? I feel I'm constantly needing to remind you I'm not fragile," said Nadala.

"I'm only wanting you to take care of yourself."

"Which is why we must keep walking," she said, moving close to the edge of the rock and peering over. She looked up, shielding her eyes with her wings to study the sky. "Things look clear now, but we've seen how quickly storms can come out of nowhere in this heat. Getting caught on this exposed rock in a storm would be dangerous. How much further until we reach the cave?"

Graxen studied the ridge across the valley, then consulted the map he'd sketched out on rawhide with a charcoal pencil. When they'd first crossed over the Cursed Mountains, they'd lucked into finding a cave with a southern facing. It had been large enough to build a fire inside without the smoke becoming overpowering, and received enough sunlight during the day to not make them depressed about the reality that they were living in a hole in the ground.

As a former messenger for the dragon king, Graxen was used to sleeping outdoors, though he'd seldom had to do so more than a few nights in a row. He'd grown up in the College of Spires, an outcast among his colleagues because of the accident of birth that had left him with pale gray scales instead of the sky blue hue proudly worn by other members of his species. Sky-dragons glorified perfection in both body and mind, and though his mind was as keen as any of his fellow dragons, and his body just as strong and swift, his freakish coloration had excluded him from both the path of scholarship and a position among the aerial guard. Messenger duty wasn't the least dignified job a dragon might be assigned to, but while sky-dragon history was full of glorifying tales of heroic guards and wise biologians, there were no hagiographies written of the lives of letter carriers.

Still, even with his low status, he'd been used to eating well prepared meals and sleeping on cushions in rooms cooled by breezes in the summer and warmed by furnaces in the winter. His duties had also allowed ample leisure time to read, a birthright of all male sky-dragons, so fundamental that even a freak such as himself had not been denied access to the libraries that dotted the kingdom. Six months into their exile in the wilderness, Graxen had learned to endure without regular meals or comfortable beds, but he grieved at the idea that he might never see a book again.

He also found it depressing that he might never see another map drawn with any degree of competence. His skills as a cartographer were somewhat lacking. The more he looked at the mountains surrounding them and compared them with the scribbles on his map, the less sure he was of where they were.

"Are we lost?" asked Nadala.

"If you mean do I know precisely where we're at in relation to the new cave, then, no, I don't, and yes, we're lost. But if you're asking in more general terms, I'm still reasonably sure we're heading in the right direction, and have hope I'll soon be able to spot a landmark I recognize. The mountains look different from the ground than from the air."

Nadala shook her head. "I'm the one who can't fly. Why you stubbornly persist in acting like your wings don't work eludes me."

"I want to be by your side in case you fall again," said Graxen.

"Again, you equate pregnancy with fragility. I'm tired. The terrain is difficult. Yes, it's not completely impossible that I might trip. When I do, it's doubtful you'll be fast enough to catch me, and I'm not so frail I can't pick myself back up. Get into the sky. Find out where we are. If it's feasible to reach the new cave before nightfall, we'll push on. If it's not, you'll need to find us shelter for the night. While you're above, keep an eye out for game. Once we eat tonight, that's the last of the meat, and neither of us will survive on berries alone."

"Of course," said Graxen. "And, while I explore, you can rest. Perhaps even catch a nap."

Nadala threw him her spear. "Very well. While I catch a nap you catch some fresh food. I don't want to have walked all this way for nothing."

"I'll do my best," he said.

"Do better than that," she said. "Remember, it's hunting, not chasing. You're fast, but game is faster among trees. Your advantage is your mind. You have to know where the prey will be before it does."

"So you've said," he said, with more strain in his voice than he intended.

"I'm sorry," she said, not sounding sorry. "Am I repeating myself? Are you tired of my advice?"

"I'm more than grateful for the advice," he said. He shook his head. "I'm only frustrated. Hunting seems to come so naturally to you, but for me—"

Nadala interrupted him with a short, joyless laugh. "Naturally? There was nothing natural about my learning to hunt. If you find my tone grating, you're fortunate you weren't taught to hunt by elder valkyries. I've never berated you, let alone beaten you, for letting your prey escape. I haven't refused to share the meat from my kills until you've caught a deer of your own."

"I'm sorry you weren't treated with more kindness in your youth," he said.

"I'm sorry you weren't treated more harshly," she said. "While I was being trained to hunt, you were likely lost in some book. If it were possible to fill our bellies with philosophy, you'd have all the skills we could wish for. Unfortunately, you won't capture a deer with some clever argument or pretty words."

"I captured you with those, didn't I?" he said, tracing his fore-talon along her cheek, just beneath the single gray scale near her eye that resembled a teardrop.

"Yes," she said, tenderly taking his talon in her own. "And I have no regrets. If I could live this past year over, I would change nothing."

"Nor I," he said. "Except I would have thrown the spear yesterday a foot to the left."

"There are other deer in the world," she said. "Bring me one."

"Yes ma'am," he said.

Graxen tossed the spear into the air, flapped his wings, and caught the weapon in his hind-talons as he rose onto the wind. He swooped out over the valley, falling slightly, gaining speed, then turned west as he started to climb higher. From the air, the terrain felt more familiar. Familiar and disappointing; they'd covered barely any distance at all on foot, three miles perhaps, five at best. The new cave was still at least fifteen miles away. There was no way they would make it tonight. With this rate of progress, even tomorrow felt doubtful.

Almost as doubtful as the odds of Graxen successfully hunting anything worth eating. When they'd first came to the mountains, Nadala had proven an able hunter. Valkyries trained in hunting deer with spears. Male sky-dragons, as a rule, saw hunting as an antique practice, not disreputable, but wholly unnecessary. The colleges were supplied with beef, pork, and poultry via farms they managed with slave labor. Nor did they customarily eat meat raw, save for fresh fish.

Graxen had been hungry enough when they first came to the forest that he'd gotten past his squeamishness about eating meat raw. Nadala had been trained to start a fire by striking a flint against her iron spearhead, but during their first week in the wild, endless rain had left absolutely nothing receptive to combustion. She'd brought down a small doe on their second night in the forest, and Graxen had found the raw meat somewhat bland and tough, but filling.

Alas, months later, he still hadn't successfully taken a deer of his own. He was fast and nimble, more agile in the air than even Nadala, but he didn't have her lifelong practice throwing a spear at a moving target. His speed and precision might have been of use if he'd ever spotted a deer in the center of a large open field, but any he saw always seemed close enough to forest lines to flee the second they caught his scent, or spotted his shadow, or heard his wings flap. Nadala could easily adjust her path so that the deer never saw, heard, or caught her scent until it was too late. The principals of doing so seemed plain enough to Graxen, but he lacked the muscle memory to pull it off. To perfectly aim his approach so that his shadow wouldn't startle the deer, he would accidentally put himself into a wind that carried his scent. If he traced the wind carefully, keeping his scent behind him, he'd try too hard to keep his path steady, flapping with a touch too much force, and the deer's ears would twitch, a prelude to bounding to safety.

When Nadala's flights became shorter and shorter as the new life within her grew larger and larger, she'd supplemented their food by catching small game with snares. Alas, the diets of two sky-dragons provided a crash course in evolution among the local fauna. Within a matter of weeks, all the prey that would fall for the snares had been caught and the rest were too skittish to take the bait. Thus, their decision to seek out new hunting grounds, despite the difficulty of the journey.

Now that he knew the cave couldn't be reached before nightfall his attention shifted to finding shelter. The sky was cloudless but the air possessed a quality, something not quite a scent and not quite a taste that made the back of his throat feel tight. The evening would bring storms.

Scanning the ridge, he spotted a rocky outcropping. He veered toward it, tilting his wings to slow his flight, surveying the rocks more closely. The space beneath the outcrop wasn't deep enough to be a cave, only going back about ten feet, and looked barely tall enough to stand under. He landed on a tree limb overlooking the entrance, studying the space more closely. It looked snaky. For much of his life, the only poisonous snakes he'd seen than been in glass cases in the College of Spires. Since they'd entered the mountains, they'd had more than a few encounters with rattlesnakes. Nadala would fearlessly kill them, making a snack of their meat. Graxen preferred to keep his distance, though at the moment he'd rather return with a snake than nothing at all.

He hopped down into the rocky shelter. He hunched over, his serpentine neck bringing his face inches from the ground as he studied a ring of rocks there. It looked almost like a fire pit. Looking up, he found the rock blackened by smoke. His heart raced. Someone was nearby! They hadn't found any signs of intelligent life since crossing into the mountains. In dragon lore, the mountains were haunted. Few dragons ventured into them, though he'd heard that some humans had villages within the mountains where they worked in mines. But they'd found no evidence of humans this far into the mountains, at least not contemporary humans. From time to time, they'd stumbled across ruins, old walls, strange bits of twisted scrap metal, broken shards of glass and pottery, evidence that someone had lived here long ago.

He studied the dusty soil beneath the outcropping and saw no sign of footprints, either dragon or human. And despite the blackened roof, there was no smell of smoke. He dug through the pale tan dirt within the stones, sifting through a few inches of soil before he found a layer of ash. This fire had been built long ago. Centuries, perhaps.

Graxen had never believed that the mountains were truly haunted. He was far too educated to believe in ghosts. But, the fact that the land had once been inhabited, and now lay so barren, hinted at some terrible, unfathomable tragedy, and made him ponder whether the danger that had driven both men and dragons from these lands might yet exist.

Whatever the danger, it wasn't here now, nor were any snakes. He leapt to the branch of the tree he'd first landed on, then threw himself out into the air, swooping down, then climbing, tracing an arc as he studied the feasibility of a pregnant dragon being able to climb up to the rocky shelter. It looked steep, but not impassible.

The journey here also looked relatively easy, since they could descend from Nadala's current position into the valley, which was broad and relatively flat. They could follow the stream and—

A flash of yellow caught Graxen's eye. Yellow was normally a color only seen in nature on flowers or dying leaves, but this hadn't been a flower. He circled back for another look.

A metal sign. Diamond shaped, about a foot tall, with a vivid yellow background and a black symbol that might have been a stylized drawing of the sun. It was a small circle surrounded by three triangles radiating away from it, their outer edges curved to trace a still larger circle.

Before he had time to ponder the meaning of the symbol, his mind latched onto an even more amazing detail. The sign was bolted to a wall, and the wall was part of a vast building almost completely hidden beneath vegetation. Now that he saw the one wall, he spotted others throughout the valley, a few at first, then hundreds, almost forming a maze, albeit one that would be easy to pass through, since most of the walls had crumbled and fallen. More yellow signs soon emerged, nearly everywhere his eyes fell now that he knew what to look for.

He landed in front of the first sign he'd spotted, which hung on the most intact building among the ruins. From above, the structure was so massive it looked like a low hill covered with trees and bushes. Parts of the outer wall had collapsed revealing three floors within. He found a door among the vines. It stood ajar. Beside it was another of the yellow sun signs. The height and location of the door hinted it had been built for humans. It was far too small to allow a sun-dragon to pass through, and, while many sky-dragon buildings had ground floor doors to accommodate human slaves, most sky-dragon structures were built many stories high, with the main door located on the highest floor and set back from a broad landing area, to allow easy takeoff and landing.

What most drew his attention was the writing. There was a sign over the door. He recognized the letters as a variant of draconic script, though far more angular and stylized. He could even make out words he recognized. O-A-K and R-I-D-G-E could be made out easily enough, though the letters had faded. The next word was long, and rust had claimed the middle letters. Assuming it was all one word, it began with an N and ended with an A-L. He could barely make out what he thought was a T about one gap away from the N. Natural? The missing gap seemed too long. Nutritional? Now the gap wasn't long enough. National? Was it even one word? Not At All might fit. The final visible word was L-A-B-O-R, though it looked like their might have been a word after that before it rusted through. He studied the faint remnants of the lost word. Stories? Perhaps this had been a training ground for slaves? Where they were taught Labor Stories? And they came from all over the kingdom to learn, making it National? As for the Oak and the Ridge, looking around it seemed an obvious place name, given the terrain and vegetation. Perhaps too obvious. It was like naming some random stretch of ocean shoreline "Sea Oats Beach." Perhaps human slaves weren't sophisticated enough for anything more poetic.

But then, how many human slaves did he know who could read? A few were taught the skill to aid the biologians, but most lacked the aptitude for learning the literary arts. The sign would be wasted on most of them.

An intriguing mystery. For upwards of thirty seconds, his mind whirred with a desire to return at once to the College of Spires and inform the historians there of his discovery. They would no doubt be eager to send a team of scholars to study the ruins. He would no longer be known as Graxen the Gray, and instead be known as Graxen the Discoverer, Revealer of Ancient Truths.

The fantasy crashed as swiftly as it took flight. He and Nadala had been banished by the Matriarch herself. If he were ever to return to the kingdom of his birth, any valkyrie or member of the aerial guard would be duty bound to put them to death on sight. If his scales had been the ordinary shade of blue, perhaps he could reach the College of Spires undetected. From a distance, it was difficult to distinguish one sky-dragon from another. With his cursed discoloration, he'd be dead within hours if he returned. There was no hope of both flying and hiding.

He pushed the door open wider and looked inside. The movement startled a nest of rats on the far side of the room, who scattered in all directions. One ran into a beam of sunlight filtering through a crack in the wall.

Before he even knew he was moving, the rat was dead, dangling at the end of the long shaft held in Graxen's fore-talons. He'd killed it! By pure reflex and instinct, he'd known where it was running and thrust his spear without even thinking of his aim.

He studied the rat closely. It was a fat little beast, with a healthy brown coat, but still only a rat, half a pound of meat at best. It was fuel for at least a few more miles walk for Nadala and the small dragon growing inside her.

NADALA COLLAPSED into the shadow beneath the overhang, panting heavily.

"By the bones," she groaned. "How do earth-dragons manage to travel everywhere on foot? I've walked more this last month than I have my whole life."

"Is your experience typical?" asked Graxen.

"Falling in love with an outcast, betraying my sisters, and being banished instead of executed because the outcast happens to be the bastard son of the all-powerful Matriarch? No. No, I would not assert that my experience is typical."

"I meant your pregnancy," he said. "You're still months from giving birth. Are other sky-dragon females normally incapacitated for so long?"

"I'm not incapacitated," she grumbled. "If anything, I'm more physically active than I've ever been in my life.

Now that I have a comparison, I can accurately say it's far easier to fly a hundred miles than it is to hike ten."

"I've chosen my words poorly," said Graxen.

"If you meant to ask if my belly has grounded me more swiftly than it grounds my pregnant sisters, I don't know. I've never spoken with a sky-dragon in the later stages of pregnancy."

"How is that possible?" Graxen asked. "The whole point of the Nest—"

Nadala raised her fore-talon, cutting him off. "I know at the College of Spires, the belief is that all female sky-dragons are preoccupied with getting pregnant, giving birth, and raising the young. The reality is, the Matriarch determines from birth, and sometimes even before birth, if we are fit for further breeding. Given my discoloration, I was deemed unfit to serve as a child-bearer and was slotted to serve solely as a warrior."

Nadala's discoloration consisted solely of a few gray scales among the tens of thousands of blue scales adorning her. She had the grey teardrop beneath her left eye, and another small batch of gray scales on her inner thighs near her genitals, which Graxen had remained unaware of even after their first few awkward attempts at mating, and noticed purely by chance after they'd bathed in a pool at the base of a waterfall and stretched out on a nearby rock to sun themselves.

He said, "But, even if you weren't meant to breed, certainly you met others who—"

"No," she said, cutting him off again. "Once a female was matched with a mate, they were isolated from the general population of the Nest, confined to the upper chambers. I would sometimes see them sunning themselves on the balconies, fat and full of life. All activity in the Nest is centered around providing for a pregnant dragon's every need. They receive the freshest meats, the choicest crops, the finest bedding, and the constant attention of a whole squadron of elder dragons who provide guidance and assurance at every stage of pregnancy. Queen Tanthia probably had more duties than a pregnant sky-dragon."

"But after they give birth and return to the normal life of the Nest—"

"They are forever apart," said Nadala, interrupting once more. Graxen clenched his jaw. He'd once overheard a human slave telling another slave that he'd lived so long with his mate that they now finished each other's sentences. Graxen felt like this only ran in one direction. Nadala interrupted him without a thought, and he would never dare to interrupt her, not because he feared her reaction, but simply because he cherished listening to her. Of course, he also cherished conversation, and was beginning to wonder if the exchange of words between them could still be categorized as such.

"You mean they never return to other duties in the Nest?" asked Graxen.

She shook her head. "It's more their attitude. They only associate with others who've given birth, though they usually return to work alongside the rest of us. Running the Nest is a laborious job, requiring all able-bodied dragons to pitch in. Unlike you males, we don't make use of slaves."

"How very liberal of you," said Graxen. A few radicals at the College of Spires viewed slavery as unjust, and he had some sympathy for their arguments, though he felt that in some ways sky-dragons were just as enslaved, given that they were assigned careers, mates, and residences by superiors who gave little regard to their preferences.

Nadala gave a brief, bitter laugh. "There's nothing liberal about our keeping humans from the Nest. They're a competitive species, desiring many of the same resources to survive and having a demonstrated propensity to gain those resources through theft, deception, and violence. Allowing such creatures inside the walls where we shelter our offspring could be the first step toward our own genocide. Besides, what need do we have of human slaves? We're experts at enslaving ourselves."

Graxen nodded. "I was thinking much the same thing."

Nadala looked out over the valley. She pointed toward something in the distance. "Is that one of them? The ruins of a human building? For a hill, it seems to have rather sharp angles."

Graxen followed her gaze. "Exactly," he said. "Once you know what to look for, they're everywhere."

"Do you think it's true?" she asked.

"What?"

"That a human civilization championed by angels existed before the dragons took control of the world?"

Graxen shrugged. "Perhaps. I've never dwelled on the question. We live in the world we were born in. What came before matters little."

"Only now we *don't* live in the world we were born in," said Nadala, softly. "We live in the wilderness, outcast and alone. I thought we'd meet others by now. I thought we'd find the dragons rumored to exist beyond the mountains. Were they only myth? What will become of our fledgling, growing up in a world all alone?"

"He or she will have us," said Graxen.

"Not forever," said Nadala. Her voice sounded grave. "In... in childbirth... sometimes a female goes into the birthing chamber and never returns. Birth... can apparently be injurious. To both the mother and the baby. And sometimes... sometimes the mother must be killed, cut open to release the baby, and save its life."

Graxen watched the birds flitting around the valley in the fading sunlight. Their songs provided an unsettling cheerful counterpoint to Nadala's heavy tone.

"It won't come that," said Graxen.

"It may," said Nadala. "And if it does, I need you—"

"It won't," he said. She looked shocked by his words, either because of his tone, more forceful than comforting, or because it was the first time in his memory that he'd cut her off midsentence. He normally hung on every word from her throat but this... this...

The bird songs seemed to mock him. How simple it must be to lay eggs, smooth, rounded, relatively small, unlike the living, rough-scaled monsters that were infant dragons, born with oversized heads sporting long jaws already filled with needle teeth.

"You must promise," she said. "You must promise to save the child."

"It won't come to that," he said, no longer forcefully, but still failing to summon a comforting tone.

"It might," she said. "And there's no point in not being prepared. If it looks as if something has gone wrong, and there's any risk of losing the baby... you need to use the spear's blade and—"

"I understand," said Graxen.

"But do you promise?"

He took a long, slow breath. "I promise," he said, looking across the valley. He saw a trio of deer far away, near the tree line. He'd never reach them before they fled. Still, the fact that they were there gave him hope.

"Let's get some sleep," he said. "We have a long way to travel in the morning. If I rise early enough, and my luck improves, we won't need to make the journey on an empty stomach."

SLEEP PROVED ELUSIVE. The heat of the day rose from the valley, turning the space beneath the rock outcropping into an oven. The storm he'd sensed earlier still hadn't arrived, though now there were distant flashes in the sky, and the low rumble of thunder rolling in from the west. When the storm arrived, it would be violent. Graxen worried whether their shelter would be sufficient.

At least, when the storm did arrive, it would finally cool the air, and hopefully provide relief for the buzzing, crackling pressure that had been growing in his skull since they'd arrived in the valley. His sick headache combined with the heat made him glad he hadn't eaten any of the rat he'd given Nadala. She needed the nourishment more than he did and, with his head throbbing like it was, he probably couldn't have kept the meal down. Plus, while Nadala hadn't been squeamish at all about eating an animal normally regarded as vermin, he suspected he'd need a few more days of hunger before he could swallow a rat, either cooked or raw.

Graxen closed his eyes, tensing the muscles in his legs and back, holding the tension, then releasing it, hoping for relaxation. He was curled up cat-like, his head resting on his tail, and though his side had grown numb he stubbornly held his position, determined by sheer force of will to break through the discomfort of his body and sleep. Nadala slept soundly. Her breathing was regular and beautiful. After their discussion earlier, the fact she was sleeping without nightmares only gave him more reason to admire her.

A loud crack echoed through the valley, followed by a sizzling sound, but, curiously, no thunder. And the flash of light was no longer a flash—even through closed eyelids, Graxen could tell the light hadn't faded. Had lightning lit a fire? He couldn't smell smoke.

Succumbing to curiosity, he opened his eyes. He found Nadala already awake, sitting on her hind-talons on a nearby boulder, spear at the ready, staring out over the valley. The valley was brightly lit, as if the sun had risen over the horizon, but from the south.

Graxen furrowed his brow. "What are we looking at?" he asked, moving to the side of the boulder.

"I was hoping you might have some clue," she said.

He didn't. He again found himself missing books more than food. Somewhere, among the nearly endless libraries of the College of Spires, some meteorologist must certainly have described all the possible types of lightning.

But what type of lightning lingered so steadily and strongly as what he now witnessed? In the valley below, from the center of the large building he'd examined earlier, a bolt of lightning crackled, dancing back and forth, arcing up to a circling cloud a few hundred feet above the rooftop. The cloud seem unconnected to the storm on the horizon, churning rapidly, but without the accompanying winds Graxen would have expected from such violent motion. He'd seen a tornado once. Its spin in retrospect was comparatively lackadaisical.

He raised his fore-talon to shield his eyes. The column of lightning was a dazzling, whitish blue. The charged sensation he'd felt in the air earlier was positively tangible now. The fringe of feathery scales along his neck ruffled involuntarily. Sparks suddenly leapt from the tip of Nadala's iron spear, striking her claw. With a cry of surprise more than pain, she dropped the weapon and leapt, landing beside him.

"Fly!" she said. "Save yourself!"

"Fly where?" asked Graxen.

"Away!" she said. "I... I don't know what this is, but fear it will destroy us both if we linger!"

"I'm not leaving you behind," said Graxen.

"I'll follow as swiftly as I can on foot," she said.

"We could try to fly together again."

"Break our necks together, you mean," she grumbled. "Just go!"

Graxen clenched his fore-talons, wondering what he could do to convince her to try flying together once more. He'd once carried his father Metron many miles on his back. Of course, his father had been old and withered, weighing half of what Nadala weighed even before her pregnancy. Female sky-dragons were slightly larger than the male of the species. And, unspoken between them was the fact that they had actually tried this once before, leaping from a much lower cliff at the edge of a lake. They hadn't quite plummeted straight down, but they also hadn't gotten very far at all before crashing into the water. On a more solid surface they might, indeed, have broken their necks.

"I'm staying," he said, firmly. "I'll not abandon you. We fear this thing because it's unknown. It may not represent a danger to us at all."

"I won't argue with you on staying," she said, recognizing the determination in his voice. "But I'm more than open to debating how dangerous this thing might be. Have you never seen what happens to a body struck by lightning?"

"I haven't, but I've also never seen lightning so confined and constant. Assuming it's lightning at all. Perhaps it's some sort of firefly mating ritual?"

"That's creating a tornado?" she asked.

Graxen hopped onto the boulder for a better view. His firefly supposition did seem unlikely and he regretted mentioning it. The initial terror of the phenomenon was fading, and curiosity was starting to overpower caution. He vaguely recalled some proverb used by human slaves involving curiosity and cats, but the exact phrasing eluded him. Did curiosity kill cats? No, that could hardly be right. To hunt, cats had to poke their noses and paws into all sort of dark nooks and crannies. Curiosity fed the cat? Though biologically accurate, that didn't sound right either.

Watching the lightning, he started a silent internal count to measure how long it would sustain itself. Should he ever again find himself in the company of biologians, he wanted to relay his observations as faithfully as possible. He studied the point where the lightning struck the rooftop. A neat, perfectly circular hole had now been carved out by the dancing arc. He tried to spot the door in the wall he'd seen earlier. The door had been about six and a half feet tall and three feet wide. He could compare the door to the size of the hole carved out by the lightning to get a better estimate of its diameter.

Only, as his eyes searched for the door, they found something far more interesting. A man! He was tall and slender, covered head to toe in tight-fitting silver armor. Indeed, the armor seemed almost like a second skin; either the man was exceedingly thin beneath the shell, or the armor was no thicker than a sheet of parchment. The protection such a flimsy film of metal could offer seemed dubious.

Even more curious than the man's attire were his actions. He held a small white rectangle in one hand—a small book perhaps—and a stubby black stylus in the other hand. A quill stripped of its feathers? He seemed to be taking notes. Then, to Graxen's great astonishment, the leaves and dirt around the man's feet suddenly burst outward in a cloud and the man flew upward, covering the thirty feet or so to the rooftop with ease. He touched down, crouching, shielding his eyes with the book, placing his other hand on the roof to steady himself. The wind might not be reaching Graxen on his perch above the valley, but apparently it was the strength of a hurricane at the epicenter.

The man crept forward, slowly, slowly, drawing nearer the lighting, still holding his book toward it, like some fairytale wizard preparing to cast a spell. For that matter, the man's silver attire reminded him of knight's armor. Wizards and knights featured prominently in the literature read to young dragons. They were always murderous villains, intent on slaying dragons for no reason other than innate evil, and were nearly always vanquished in the final pages by some clever stratagem of the heroic young dragon whose name adorned the cover of the book.

Graxen had viewed those long ago tales as nothing but fantasy and had never believed in wizards, despite the well-known fact that King Albekizan had one in his employ. Vendevorex, Master of the Invisible, was a fellow sky-dragon, but one looked upon by most scholars at the College of Spires as a fraud. Still, if ever there were a phenomenon before his eyes that argued for the existence of magic, this was it.

Whatever the man was doing with his book, he seemed to have finished. He turned and crab walked back toward the edge of the roof. With a sudden rupture, a portion of the roof collapsed and the man dropped into the hole, losing his grip on this book, which blew away in the wind.

Graxen looked back to Nadala. "Did you see—?"

"The man, yes," she called back. "What was he doing? What was it he dropped?"

"I'm going to find out," said Graxen, spreading his wings.

"Graxen, no!" Nadala cried, but he plunged forward as if he hadn't heard her. He understood the insanity of his actions. If the wizard-knight had dropped a sword, or a staff, or even a bag filled with gold, he wouldn't have leapt. But a book! On the off chance the fall hadn't killed the human, he had to reach the book before the man did.

His flight proved much swifter than he'd anticipated. The relatively still air higher in the valley gave way to a growing inrush of wind. From the man's actions, he'd assumed the wind was blowing away from the lightning, but now it seemed that the lightning was aggressively sucking in all the atmosphere it could.

Graxen's years of navigating the skies served him well. He adjusted the angle of his flight into an aggressive dive, his wings tight against his body, until he'd gained enough speed that when he spread his wings again he caught onrushing air despite the terrible backwind. Wings wide, he drifted down to land near the fallen book.

His heart sank as he retrieved the object from the bush where it had fallen. It wasn't a book, but some sort of thin, rectangular tablet, like a tiny portable writing desk. It was crafted from some smooth white substance Graxen couldn't quite identify. Porcelain? Glass? Enameled metal? The back was featureless save for a small black circle ringed with silver around a tiny glass window revealing an even smaller glass bead within. The front of the tablet was a sheet of glass filled glowing with its own internal light. Words, numbers, and symbols danced beneath the glass, but, though he could read the letters, the words seemed like nonsense, randomly strung together syllables like something out of *The Ballad of Belpantheron*. What was a neutrino? What was a tachyon? What did the dancing bars beside each word indicate?

"I'll take that back now, if you don't mind," said a voice behind him.

He turned to find the wizard-knight standing near. Up close, the impression that the man wore armor turned out to be exaggerated. As near as Graxen could tell, the silver was actually painted onto the man, revealing every sculpted detail of his muscles. He looked utterly hairless, lacking even eyebrows. He also, despite his lack of pants, showed no signs of genitalia. What a strange creature. And, stranger still...

"You're not breathing," said Graxen. Despite the roaring wind above him, he could see that the man's chest didn't rise and fall, nor did his nostrils give any hint of movement. Indeed, the man was strangely devoid of any scent at all.

"And you're not handing me back my tablet," said the man. "Look, I've never met one of you before, but from everything I've read I'm guessing you're a sky-dragon. They say you're pretty intelligent."

"Who are they?" asked Graxen.

"The e-lunatics!" said the man, sounding pleased. He gave a slight chuckle. "My, uh, team. We live on the moon." Despite the lack of hair, he scratched the back of his head. "That must sound pretty crazy to you."

"About what I'd expect from a lunatic."

"See, we aren't actual lunatics. We're e-lunatics. It's a play on my name and our mission and what naysayers called our team when we went up to build the colony, and oh my God, why are we discussing this? Just give me back my tablet!"

"Who are you?" asked Graxen. "Why are you doing this?"

"This?"

Graxen nodded toward the shaft of lightning.

"Right. This. I've… I think I might have torn a hole in time. An honest mistake. I'm Joseph Elijah. I don't know if that name means anything to you since it's been a long time since I've walked the earth, but back in the day people said I was the smartest man alive. I need that data you're holding onto right now, or some seriously terrible stuff might happen." Elijah held out his hand, palm up.

Graxen took a step backward. The rumors that the mountains were haunted suddenly didn't seem as impossible as they once had. Here was a man with no breath, no scent, who claimed not to have walked the earth in a long time. Graxen wasn't inclined to keep property that didn't belong to him, but he also wasn't certain that aiding this unliving thing was a wise course of action. He said, "What do you mean by terrible stuff?"

"Best case scenario, I don't know, the rip in time starts spitting out dinosaurs? Dinosaurs if we're lucky. Primordial viruses nothing alive will have a defense against if we're not as lucky? Worst case scenario, the time rip turns into a space rip and the planet gets torn right down the middle, ending all life as we know it. There's a little wiggle room in my calculations. Now hand over that tablet before I do something we'll both regret!"

"Are you threatening me?" asked Graxen, holding up his fore-talon so that his sharp claws caught the light. He wasn't violent by habit, but he suspected he could make short work of the man if they came to blows, especially since the man seemed to be unarmed, and, in his unclothed state, there was certainly no place he could comfortably be concealing a blade. The talk about time rips and dinosaurs struck him as the babbling of a self-confessed madman. Or mad ghost, or whatever he was. The fact that ghosts and wizards and knights were unflinchingly evil in every story he'd ever read gave him a gut feeling that he'd be a lunatic himself to hand this seemingly magical tablet back so that the wizard-knight-ghost could finish whatever terrible spell he was casting.

Elijah pressed his left fist into his right palm. When he pulled his hands apart, the left fist had sprouted four parallel knives at least twelve inches long and wickedly sharp. "If it's a claw contest you want to get into, I'm afraid you'll lose."

"How about a contest of flight?" asked Graxen, kicking off, flapping his wings, spinning into the wind. The tailwind that had nearly crashed him was now a headwind. Gaining altitude in a good strong headwind was something even a leaf could do. He sailed higher on the wind, already planning the path he would follow into the forests across the valley. He assumed the moon-ghost would chase him into the forest, while Graxen would double back to Nadala and together they would flee.

There was a loud *WHOOOMPH* below, and he glanced down to see the man rocketing skyward, his knife arm outstretched before him, turning his whole body into a deadly projectile. His speed made him nearly impossible to outrun, but a human body wasn't built for maneuverability in the air. Graxen wheeled away, leaving Elijah to slice through empty sky. The silver man made a wide arc back around to attack again, still moving fast, but, as Graxen had suspected, his motions lacked finesse. His path seemed wobbly, buffeted by wind, and Graxen deliberately let him draw near, then dove. This close, the man had no time to react. Graxen corkscrewed in the air, turning his hind-talons up, using them to rake the man's torso, to no effect. The man's thin silver shell deflected Graxen's claws as effectively as if he'd been wearing plate mail. At least the man was, indeed, solid. Perhaps he wasn't a ghost, and his initial instinct that the moon-man was a wizard had validity.

Graxen took a deep breath as he spun back to level off his flight. He swerved again as the man raced up behind him, slicing the air where Graxen had just been. Graxen felt the first stirrings of panic. Of course the moon-wizard couldn't be hurt. Obviously the man wore enchanted armor. Perhaps he should drop the tablet, and hope the man no longer gave chase. But Elijah had all but confessed that the lightning vortex was his creation, and seemed to regard the tablet as essential to controlling it. It still felt foolish to give him what he wished, but what if he had no choice? While Graxen could elude the silver man for quite some time, his hide most certainly wasn't enchanted. Eventually the man's blades would draw blood, he would die, and Nadala...

Nadala.

His instincts had been to keep her safely away from the moon-man. What if, as was often the case involving Nadala, his instincts were wrong?

He rose higher, toward the swirling vortex of clouds. Now that he'd had more time to study the leaves and debris swirling around him, he saw that the inrushing winds change into outflowing winds at the top and bottom of the vortex. He rode the hurricane winds dizzily around the lightning, then spun off, faster than he'd ever flown before, heading straight for the rock shelter where he'd left Nadala. There was no chance she hadn't watched his encounter with the wizard-knight. Graxen swerved at the last second as the silver man raced at him from behind, slashing the air with his blades. He'd sensed the man's approach by the faintest tingle in his tail as the cone of air pushed by the man's body had tickled the tip. A half second slower and he'd have been sliced to ribbons.

As Nadala had counseled earlier, there was chasing, and there was hunting. He was done with being chased. It was time to turn this into a hunt. The bright, dancing lightning directly behind him cast his shadow forward, darkening the interior of the cave. He didn't see Nadala within. Had she fled?

No. She'd seen him coming toward the cave, silver man in pursuit, and hidden herself. And there was only one place that made sense to hide.

With hard, rapid wing beats that made his heart feel like it would burst, he flew straight at the rocks. As he reached the boulder that lay not far from the entrance, he wheeled, darting around it, folding his wings tightly as he hurtled through the enclosed space of the shelter, then spreading his wings again as he flashed back into open air.

Behind him in heard a loud grunt and a sharp CLANG! He wheeled around to see Nadala standing over the man, who was pinned to the ground, face down. Her spear had gone right through the center of his lower spine and pinned him like an insect in a display case. The soles of his silver feet still kicked up dust for a few seconds, then died off. He slid down the shaft of the spear, lying motionless in the dirt. Graxen flapped to return to the shelter, landing before the fallen man.

"Who and what and how and why?" Nadala asked, in an animated tone.

"Elijah. Moon-wizard? Magic! He's evil?" answered Graxen, with a confused shrug. "It happened very fast."

"And you just trusted I'd kill him if you steered him my direction?" she asked, her voice trembling with energy.

"Yes," he said. "I felt quite certain of it."

She relaxed. "That is the most romantic thing you've ever said to me. It makes me miss when we wrote love letters to one another. Telling me you had faith I could kill even a moon-wizard would have been quite flattering."

"I'm not dead," said Elijah, raising himself onto his elbows. "Fun as it was chasing you, why don't you give me the tablet now?"

"What tablet?" asked Nadala.

Graxen held it up. "He used it to cast a spell to make the lightning. I think."

"That is wrong in so many ways I don't even know where to start," said the silver man. He twisted his neck. He seemed to be in no pain from the spear that had pierced him. Graxen smelled no blood, nor any hint of bodily waste that one would normally expect from such an injury. "First, though, introductions. I'm Joseph Elijah. Last time I was around these parts, they called me the Moon Man."

"I'm Nadala," said Nadala. "This is my mate, Graxen. What manner of man are you that you can survive such injuries?"

"A man who's already survived his own death," said Elijah. "A thousand years ago, I perfected the world's first permanent transplantable artificial heart. It made me a wealthy man. Wealthy enough that I bought the Maldives, which were in imminent danger of vanishing beneath a rising ocean. Luckily, the Dutch figured out how to beat a rising ocean a long time ago. Once I used my fortune to save the nation, I started my own space program and built a colony on the moon without any of the red tape I'd have had to cut through if I'd remained in America. It was a profitable venture, since only billionaires could afford to settle there. And the only thing I enjoyed more than being rich was being alive, so as various body parts failed, I replaced them, building on the tech I'd developed for my artificial heart and borrowing heavily from already existing patents on artificial limbs. Eventually…" he rapped his temple with his silver knuckles. "…even my brain got replaced. There's a direct correlation between the Joseph Elijah born in San Francisco in 2015 and the man I am today. The funny thing is, my new body could shrug it off if you'd shot me or shocked me or gone at me with your teeth. But I honestly didn't plan for a spear attack. Even a genius can't plan for everything."

Graxen eyed Nadala. "I should also have warned you he's a lunatic."

"That's an e-lunatic," said Elijah, shaking his head. "And I'm not crazy. Look, I know we lack a common vocabulary to really discuss this situation, but—"

"Your draketongue is very good," said Nadala, reassuringly.

"I'm not speaking draketongue, you're speaking English," said Elijah. "Because the first dragon was an American invention and holy shit I still can't believe we're jabbering about trivia when the world is about to get ripped in half!"

Nadala gave Graxen a worried glance. "Are you certain he's a lunatic?"

"He might also be a ghost. Or a wizard. Or a knight. Or all three."

"Knights are the good guys, right?" asked Elijah, hopefully.

"Not any I've heard of," said Nadala.

"Get this spear out of me and give me the damned tablet!" Elijah screamed, beating the ground with his fists like a child throwing a tantrum. "We're seriously on the verge of complete and total destruction if you don't let me go right now!"

Nadala furrowed her brow and grasped the spear shaft with both talons.

"Don't," said Graxen.

"Do you have a plan to get rid of that hell storm out in the valley?" she asked.

"No," said Graxen.

"Yes," said Elijah.

"That's what I thought," said Nadala, yanking the shaft free. "I'm already worried about giving birth so far from my sisters. The thought of raising a daughter or son in a world ripped in two is something I'd rather not have hanging over my head."

Elijah rolled over onto his back. "Thank you." He lifted his arm straight up. "I'll need a minute while my system repairs itself. While we wait, let me look over the data I collected."

Nadala nodded toward Graxen, who handed him the tablet.

Elijah's silver lips bent into a frown as he looked at the screen. "Well, great."

"What's great?" asked Graxen.

"The mass readings. And they aren't great. They're terrible. Something huge came through the time rift while I was wasting time with you. Nine tons. I was just joking about the dinosaur earlier but apparently the universe doesn't understand my sense of humor. Not that you'd know what the hell a dinosaur is."

"Of course I know what a dinosaur is," said Graxen. "The halls of the biologians are filled with fossils. We dragons are the descendants of the tyrant lizards who once ruled this world."

Elijah chuckled. "That is one messed up creation myth but, you know, it's no dumber than the stupid things people believed. Anyway, if we're lucky, something big with a duck bill slipped through the rift. If we're not as lucky, it's something with teeth far longer than anything you've ever seen."

"I've seen sun-dragons," said Graxen. "And the skull of tyrannosaurus rex. Its teeth were as long as your knuckle blades."

"Sounds like your biologians went shopping in the ruins of the Museum of Natural History," said Elijah, sitting up. "Okay, this really isn't how I planned to die, but I think I've got what I need. I can program the power plant at the base of my skull into a makeshift bomb. I just need to jump into the rift and blow it up." He sighed. "Man, I should have listened to Isis."

"Who's Isis?" asked Nadala.

"My wife. At least, she used to be. She told me to stay the hell away from Oak Ridge. But I slipped off and came here anyway. You see, about a thousand years ago, Oak Ridge housed a research facility that did cutting edge science. The published stuff was impressive, but the black book stuff was even crazier. There were whispers they were taking apart an alien ship here. Maybe even actual aliens. They were also looking into teleportation. Telepathy. Alternate reality gates. Clones. And, you know, cybernetics." He held up his metal hand. "Real comic book stuff. And surprisingly well built. Apparently some of the big red buttons with a hundred warning symbols around them still turn on stuff if you push them."

He rose. "Repairs are done. Great talking to you. Dragons! Who said the apocalypse wouldn't come with a side of whimsy."

"I don't understand half the things you're saying," said Nadala.

"Half?" asked Graxen.

"Not important. I'm talking just to hear myself talk. Old habit of mine. Or I guess, if a habit's stuck around a thousand years, it's not a habit anymore. It's who you are. Or maybe it's just a tiny glitch in the quantum processor housing my consciousness. Who the hell can tell?" He shrugged.

Graxen and Nadala shrugged back.

"It's been real," said Elijah. He gave Nadala a crisp salute. "By the way, would you look after this for me?"

He handed Nadala a tiny wafer, no bigger than a coin, but thinner.

"What's this?" she asked.

"Nothing you need to worry about," he said. "If anyone comes looking for me, though, promise you'll give them this, okay?"

"Very well," she said.

"And keep that spear handy in case it was a t-rex. Though, what are the odds? I mean, one dinosaur slips through and it just happens to be one everybody's heard of? On the other hand, given the long odds of anything at all getting fossilized, maybe they weren't all that rare. I'd still get the hell out of here, dinosaur or no. This whole place is radioactive out to about three or four miles. Now, if you'll excuse me, I'm off to save reality!"

Elijah launched into the air with a *swoosh* and a backwash of dust and grit.

"That was... odd," said Nadala, studying the tip of her spear. "Between your poor hunting and my driving the tip through a metal man and six inches into the ground, this thing might not last much longer."

"You can't sharpen it?"

"I'll keep sharpening it, but the blade is getting stress fractures. Sooner or later, it will fail."

She flinched as a clap of thunder shook the mountainside. The valley grew suddenly dark. The lightning column was gone.

"He did it!" said Graxen. "Whatever it was he was doing."

"What does radioactive mean?" asked Nadala.

"I have no idea. But the cave we're heading to lies well beyond the radius of three or four miles."

"Then let's get going," said Nadala.

"Now? In the dark? With a storm coming on?"

"I'll survive a little rain," she said, looking at the now dark landscape.

Graxen looked out over the darkened valley. The storm seemed to have lost its energy, perhaps sucked of its heat by the vortex, but thick clouds and smoke from the smoldering ruins made it impossible to see more than a few yards. With no moon and stars, it was dark as a tomb. If there was a dinosaur out there, it could be hiding anywhere. It could be looking at them right now, in fact.

"I'm not going to be able to sleep anyway," he said, stuffing their few belongings into the leather satchel. "Let's get going."

DAWN FOUND THEM many miles away. Graxen had grown disoriented in the moonless darkness and was greatly relieved when the sun rose at their backs. The relief brought by the sun confirming his sense of direction turned into crushing weariness as the sun burned away the morning clouds and began to bake the landscape. Given their reptilian heritage, most dragons enjoyed sunbathing, but not while hiking, and most definitely not while on the verge of collapse from hunger and exhaustion.

"Are you all right?" Nadala asked as Graxen grabbed the trunk of a narrow tree and used it to steady himself.

"I'm feeling a little weak," he confessed. "Is there any deer jerky left?"

"I finished it off yesterday before I even reached the shelter. You can't believe how grateful I was you captured that rat."

Graxen nodded. Yesterday, he'd wondered how hungry he would have to be to eat a rat. The answer, it seemed, was one sleepless night's hike hungrier.

"Let's go down to the creek," said Nadala. "Perhaps I can spear some fish."

"Perhaps," said Graxen, though fish of decent size were few and far between in these shallow, rocky streams. Still, a few minutes overturning rocks in shallow water would yield crawfish and snails. The effort spent in collecting them was barely more than the energy spent, but he would... he would...

... and then he was on the ground, wondering *why* he was on the ground.

He was vaguely, distantly aware he'd been snoring, then decided not to fight it, and gave in to sleep.

HE WOKE IN MID-AFTERNOON. He sat up, bleary-eyed.

"What's that smell?" was the first thing he asked.

"Good morning to you too," said Nadala, sitting beside him beneath the shade of a giant oak.

Graxen sat up, sniffing the air.

"Urine?" he said, though he wasn't sure why he said the word as a question. The scent reminded him of the piss of ox dogs, or perhaps sun-dragons. Some large beast with nothing but raw meat in its diet.

"Must be," said Nadala. "It's pretty strong when the breeze comes from the east. A bear marking its territory, perhaps? Or wolves?"

Or a dinosaur, thought Graxen, though he didn't dare say it out loud.

"Whatever it is, we should get moving," said Graxen.

"Whatever it is, we should kill it," said Nadala. "After this hike, I can confidently say that when we reach the cave, I'm staying there until I give birth. If it's this wearisome to hike now, I can't imagine what it will be like a month from now. We'll be living in the new cave a long time. I'd rather not have a pack of wolves or a hungry bear sniffing around when I'm caring for an infant."

"Do you want me to track down the smell right now?" asked Graxen.

"Right now," she said, "I want you to eat your fish." She pointed toward two middling pan fish barely bigger than the leaves they were laying on. "Then, I want you to lead on to the cave. I don't feel like I can rest until we've reached it."

"I'm looking forward to reaching it as well," said Graxen. "It's a nice cave. For a cave. Perhaps, if the area proves fertile, I could build a less gloomy structure. I've seen the log cabins built by humans. They seem... achievable. Not easy, but doable."

"We'll have to do it without the spear," she said, her voice cracking. She held up the shaft. The tip was missing three inches. "It snapped when I was fishing. It... was only a matter of time." Her eyes were moist. "I've... I've used this spear a long time. It's almost like losing a friend."

Graxen nodded. It felt even more like losing the one piece of civilization that still stood between them and death in the savage wild. But perhaps it was best not to share this feeling. It was also probably best not to express relief that the spear had finally broken when she'd been using it, not him. More and more, Graxen felt like the secret to a smooth and happy relationship with his mate was mastering the art of what not to say.

DESPITE HIS EXHAUSTION, Graxen woke before dawn on his first night in the cave, his hunger gnawing his gut like a living thing. Nadala was still sleeping. Graxen studied her with concern. She seemed dead to the world, not reacting at all to the crunching of his claws in the gravel as he rose. He had to lean close to confirm she was breathing. Her face and shoulders looked thinner than they once did. Her belly was larger, but it seemed that her body was consuming itself to feed the growing life inside her.

No more. It was time to hunt. It was time for him to prove himself capable of caring for his mate. Their months in exile had been marked by distinct stages. At first, Nadala had mourned their exile. Then, she began to trust him, to view him as a worthy companion on their journey into the unknown. Then had come the intimacy, and the happiness, and the feeling that they were mastering their new life. But ever since she'd realized she was pregnant, his failings had come into sharper view. Whether or not she had doubts about his worthiness as a mate, his self-doubt grew with each failed hunt. Catching rats and snakes wasn't enough. It was time to bring down a deer.

He walked to the mouth of the cave. From here, he could see the field where he'd spotted the stag a few evenings before. He'd been unable to kill the stag with a spear. But what if the spear had been a flaw in his hunting strategy all along? Nadala had trained with it so long the spear was like part of her body. A few months of practice wouldn't make him her equal. Graxen had trained his body for flight all his life. Without the spear, he felt certain he would have cleared the field a fraction of a second faster, reaching the deer before it reached the forest. His claws had failed to intimidate Elijah, but they weren't just for show. They were sharp enough to rip flesh.

Now he just needed to find flesh to rip.

He took to the air as the sun crept over the horizon, casting long shadows through the fog that hung over the meadow. He swooped around to the western edge of the field, so that his shadow would fall over the open space. The air was still; perhaps his scent wouldn't carry far. Or perhaps his scent would be obscured by the nearly overpowering stench that hung over the forest, the predator urine stink they'd detected the day before, now amplified by the damp air, and, perhaps, closer proximity? If there was a pack of wolves, how could he handle them? One on one, he didn't feel like a wolf would prove a threat. But a large pack? Without a spear, they might prove challenging.

This morning, however, his focus wasn't on the predators that he might be in competition with. He needed to be single-minded in pursuit of prey. Almost as if willing it made it so, as he circled back from the forest toward the field he saw the stag in the company of three does on the far side of the meadow. They were spread out within the high grass, fifty yards or so from the edge of the forest. Their heads were held high, but they weren't looking toward him. Their gaze was fixed upon the forest behind them.

There was no time to plan, only to act. The fact there were four deer gave him four targets, but also four times the odds that he would be spotted. A small doe was closest, but the stag wasn't far behind her, and would provide far more meat. None of the deer had even glanced his way. All still stared intently at the forest. This was his chance! He swooped in, gaining speed, then tilted up, bringing his hind-talons down, the fading mist beneath him swirling. A bare second before he reached the stag, the animal bolted, turning 180 degrees in a single heartbeat and leaping with all its might straight at Graxen. Graxen rose swiftly, avoiding a high speed collision with the antlers, which would certainly injure him, if not outright kill him.

He glanced around desperately, searching for another target. All the deer were in panicked flight away from the trees, out into the meadow. He still stood a chance. But before he could give chase, his eyes caught the movement of swaying trees, followed swiftly by loud crashing and snapping. The treetops trembled. To his astonishment, an enormous, bipedal lizard at least twenty feet tall leapt from the forest, charging into the field in pursuit of the deer with an earsplitting roar. Graxen beat his wings for all he was worth, rising higher, hoping the beast truly was pursuing the deer and not him. Fortunately, the creature seemed to have his attention fixed on the deer. In fact, he seemed to be in pursuit of the stag. Graxen's stag. Graxen furrowed his brow. Should he fly away and let this thing eat its fill?

No.

Nadala hadn't wanted a bear or a wolf for a neighbor. There was no way they could share their hunting grounds with this thing, and no way he was going to go back to the cave and tell Nadala they had to move again.

Graxen was now high enough he had no fear that the creature could leap up and snatch him. Not that the creature looked capable of much in the way of a vertical leap, despite legs thick as tree trunks. The thing was much longer than a sun-dragon from snout to tail, and far more massive. Its long, thick tail alone probably weighed more than even the largest sun-dragons. Was this a tyrannosaurus rex? He'd only seen fossils and the drawings reconstructing them. Unlike the drawings, this beast had a leonine mane, though it sported dark red feathers instead of fur. Below the neck, its skin was scaly, a mottled green and rust color that no doubt camouflaged it well in the thick of the forest.

Its muscles seemed designed for one purpose: outsprinting prey. Despite the stag's impressive speed, it had to leap over brush, and bound from side to side to avoid thorny thickets. The dinosaur ran straight as an arrow, trampling bushes, ignoring the veers of the stag, somehow seeming to know exactly where the stag would be once it closed the gap.

With a fresh burst of speed, the creature opened its jaws wide. It looked capable of swallowing an ox-dog. It teeth clamped onto the stag's hindquarters. The deer screamed, a shrill, shrieking, rabbit-like cry that curdled Graxen's blood. Until this moment, he hadn't known deer could make such noise.

The cry came to an abrupt end as the dinosaur whipped the stag back and forth like a cat savaging a mouse. When the head whipping stopped, the stag looked limp and broken. The dinosaur let the lifeless mass drop from its jaws, then sniffed the body, as if for the first time pondering just what it was it had caught.

Graxen gathered his courage and decided to get the beast's attention before it gulped down any of the stag's valuable meat.

"Yaaaah!" he screamed, swooping right at the dinosaur. The great beast lifted its head, its small, dark eyes looking puzzled. Graxen swooped over the dinosaur's snout. He looked back over his shoulder and saw the creature's head turned toward him, tracking his motion.

Graxen took a measure of inspiration from the fact that the giant predator had acted a bit like a cat in finishing off the stag. Like a cat, its attention seemed easily drawn to movement. Graxen circled back, drawing even closer this time. The beast opened its jaws and snapped at him, far too slow. Graxen didn't have to look back as he headed for the trees across the field. He could hear the beast's massive feet thundering through the brush as it gave chase. Graxen flew as slow as he dared, to tease the creature on. When the noise behind him grew too close for comfort, he responded with a fresh burst of speed.

Graxen reached the forest. This was old growth, as open and expansive as a cathedral once you made it past the smaller trees near the edge. It was dangerous for him to fly in the confined space, especially in such unfamiliar territory. But, if the territory was unfamiliar to Graxen, it was equally unfamiliar to the dinosaur. The beast crashed through the forest boundary and thundered into the open space beneath the older trees. Of course, open was a relative term. For a creature who could fly, the fallen, dead trees throughout the forest provided no barrier, nor did the huge piles of rocks that scattered the forest. The dinosaur leapt over the first of these obstacles, but, with its focus on Graxen, it soon stumbled when crossing a fallen log, though without falling. Still, its momentum was gone, and it seemed to forget the chase. It looked around in bewilderment, as if lost.

Graxen lighted in a branch. It would be a simple matter to climb up through the canopy and fly back to the fallen stag, tearing off as much meat as he could manage before the dinosaur found its way back. His earlier musings about how his claws were adequate for killing a deer gave way to calculations that he had no chance at all of inflicting genuine harm on this beast, even though it was now standing still, panting heavily, its lungs like bellows. The thing's body seemed built for speed, not endurance.

If Graxen had the spear, he could have tried to pierce the creature's hide. Without the spear, what could he use for a weapon? The only thing around were rocks and branches. Very well. He might be a poor marksman with a spear, but he could certainly drop a rock. He spied a pile of stone a few dozen yards distant. He flapped to it and selected a stone the size of a melon, weighing fifteen pounds, perhaps twenty.

The dinosaur watched him carefully. Drawing on some hidden reserve of energy, it charged. Graxen feared for a moment he'd miscalculated. With the stone, he couldn't fly as fast, and he certainly wasn't as agile maneuvering among the trees. But the weary predator was even less agile. It tripped over the very pile of stones where Graxen had been standing, caught off guard by a hidden hole left where a root had rotted away. Before it could rise, Graxen flew to the tallest branch of the tree above. He was directly over the beast's head, which opened its mouth and looked up to roar at him.

Graxen dropped the stone. From fifty feet in the air, a heavy stone could bury itself in dense soil. The creature proved sturdier than soil, but as the stone bounced off the monster's snout it took a portion of hide with it, leaving the creature bleeding. Graxen swooped to another rock pile, finding a stone of a similar size. By now the dinosaur was back on its feet, shaking its head, grunting. It snorted, then sneezed, sending a trail of bloody snot across the forest floor. Graxen flew right at the beast, gaining speed. The creature turned toward him, but not fast enough. Graxen let go of the rock only inches from the beast's eye. It hit with a satisfying crack and the creature howled in pain. Graxen landed on a tall branch and looked back to see what damage he'd inflicted. The wounded eye was on the opposite side of the beast, but he could see blood dripping freely on to the litter beneath the behemoth. Had he half blinded it? Did it matter? The creature's skull was thick enough to withstand a direct hit with a heavy rock or two. But what about four, or five? Ten? A hundred? The creature was injured and wearied, the dull look in its gaze hinted it was ill equipped to face a foe with the intelligence of a dragon. Graxen drew a deep breath, contemplating the task before him. The creature wasn't the only one who was weary. Perhaps the wise thing to do would be to leave. Pressing his attack while tired would only put him in greater and greater danger.

But, there was Nadala to consider, and their unborn son or daughter.

He would do what needed to be done. He opened his wings and once more glided to a pile of stones. He selected the heaviest one yet, and climbed with effort into the air. When he wheeled around to where he'd hit the beast the last time, he saw the eye was already swollen shut, and the hard round disc that he supposed to be the dinosaur's ear was bleeding. With all his might, he bashed the heavy stone against the injured ear without letting go. The beast let out a moan and stumbled, its legs buckling. Graxen flapped hard, panting for breath, and circled back once more. The beast was struggling to rise as he smashed the stone into the orbit of the already injured eye. The creature crashed onto its side, thrashing its tail, its feeble, tiny fore-claws opening and closing helplessly.

Its chest heaved. It no longer tried to rise. Graxen landed in a tree directly above. He let go of the stone. This time, it made a wet sound as it crashed into the dinosaur's skull, and when it bounced away it left a visible indentation.

The creature voided its bladder. Graxen now knew for certain the source of the scent that had haunted the valley earlier. He took a long, deep breath of the foul air. Was the creature dying? Its breaths were ragged, irregular. Wearily, Graxen dropped down for another stone. As long as he could hear it breathing, his work wasn't done.

THE SUN WAS SETTING as Graxen dragged the buck up the steep slope leading to the cave. He'd been gone all day. It had taken thirteen stones to finally silence the beast, and in the aftermath he'd been too weary to fly. He'd also lost his way in the shadows of the forest, and had taken hours to find his way back to the field. His search for the stag had been facilitated by the buzzards circling overhead.

"Graxen," said Nadala, perched on a boulder near the mouth of the cave. "I take it you killed the dinosaur?"

He looked up at her. "How did—"

"The thing was hardly silent when it came roaring into the field. It woke me. I saw you lead it into the forest. I heard much of the fight that followed."

"Were you worried?" he asked.

"No," she said.

Graxen thought this was a bit callous, but held his tongue. She disappeared from the rock. A cascade of loosed gravel came down the path as she slid down the slope to join him. She eyed the stag with cool eyes. "Pity the hindquarter got so mangled." She grabbed a leg and said, "Hurry. You can't believe how famished I am."

Curiously, though he'd been absolutely starved this morning, he'd forgotten his hunger while killing the dinosaur. He'd felt his hunger rise while searching for the stag, but had lost it again at the sight of all the flies covering the bloodied carcass.

Nadala grunted as she strained to pull the deer higher up the slope. Graxen pushed as best he could, but he had little strength left. It was dark by the time they reached the cave. Graxen collapsed to the floor, panting. Nadala had built a fire in his absence. It had already warmed the cave and chased away much of the dampness. She'd also gathered leaves and grass and covered them with buckskin to make crude beds. He appreciated the gesture, but felt too tired to crawl onto one.

"Was it a tyrannosaurus?" asked Nadala.

"It may have been," said Graxen. "Once the buzzards pick the flesh off the skull I may recognize it better."

Nadala had taken the whetstone from the pack and started sharpening the spearhead. Even broken, the blade would remove the hide from the deer far more effectively than their claws, and keep more of it intact for future use.

"Not even a little?" he asked.

"Worried?" she asked.

"Yes," he said.

"A little," she admitted. "But... you're Graxen the Gray. The first time we met, I chased you and you eluded me. The dinosaur had no hope of catching you."

"I could have escaped it easily," he said. "But how did you know I'd kill it?"

"Because," she said, sliding the spearhead against the stone. "I told you to. Yesterday. I thought it was a bear then, of course. But, I had faith in you."

"More faith than I have in myself, perhaps," said Graxen. "I still haven't technically successfully hunted a deer."

"Do you think dinosaur is edible?" she asked.

"We'll find out, I imagine."

"Graxen," she said, putting down the stone and spear. She came to his side and curled up next to him on the ground, her body hot against his. "I'm sorry if I've been hard on you."

"Don't be," he said.

"I wouldn't be hard if I didn't believe in you. I wouldn't be pregnant if I didn't believe you were a worthy mate. Always remember that. If I'm sometimes terse, or harsh—"

"You are the whetstone," said Graxen. "I am the blade."

"We are the whetstone," she said. "We are the blade. Together, we shall be sharp enough to carve a home from this wilderness. Do you believe in me?"

"Yes," he whispered.

"Then you believe in yourself," she said, nuzzling her cheek to his. "Welcome to our home, Graxen."

"Welcome to our home, Nadala," he said, as the stars grew crisp in the cooling night.

HAUNTED

HAUNTED

THERE'S A DRAGON in the henhouse," said Zeeky, looking up from the candlelit page before her.

Bitterwood gazed at her wearily from the bed, half asleep, wondering if she'd actually spoken or if he'd dreamt the words.

Zeeky tilted her head to the side, a look of concentration on her face. "Three of them, sounds like." The two dogs by her feet lifted their heads, sniffing the air.

Bitterwood rose with a groan, fumbling in the shadows next to his bed for his boots. His body ached from the day's labor. He and Jeremiah had spent most of the afternoon repairing the stone fence that ran along the eastern boundary of his farm. The boy slumbered soundly, snoring, oblivious to Zeeky's words. Jeremiah didn't even stir when the dogs rose, barking as they ran to the door.

"You don't have to go out," said Zeeky, rising from her chair. "They'll run when they hear Nut and Catfish coming." She pulled the wooden peg that held the door shut. The door cracked open and the two dogs shot through, baying loudly, sounding joyous as they bolted into the moonless dark of the summer night.

"It's not enough that they run," Bitterwood said, pulling on his boots, his weariness leaving him with each heartbeat. Dragons! He'd heard about raids on neighboring farms, but so far they'd stayed clear of his land. "They'll try again another night, or go down the road to the widow's farm and kill her chickens, or worse."

"It's just some old tatterwings," said Zeeky, stepping out into the yard. She had his dark brown cloak draped over her shoulders, so that in the dim starlight it looked as if her head with its bright blond hair was floating, disembodied.

"You see them?" Bitterwood asked, taking his bow down from the wall. He could see in the dark better than most men, but was no match for Zeeky. The girl's senses bordered on the supernatural. She could read the body language of animals with such eerie precision it was like she could converse with them, and, as had just been proven, not even the dogs could match her in filtering out odd noises from the normal background symphony of bugs and frogs and the breeze rustling through the corn.

Zeeky shook her head "I didn't see them, just heard them, and I've lost track now that the dogs are making such a racket. They hightailed it for the creek, but I'm not sure if they crossed it."

"How do you know it's tatterwings?" he asked.

"The way their claws sounded on the ground. Tatterwings don't hop as much as other sky-dragons."

Bitterwood had spent twenty years hunting dragons and thought he knew all there was to know about them, but he'd never noticed this detail. Not that he'd spent much time hunting tatterwings. These were outcast sky-dragons, their wings slashed by brother dragons as punishment for crimes. They were so pathetic it was almost more cruel to let them live, but he couldn't turn a blind eye to their theft.

"They only got a couple of chickens," said Zeeky, as Bitterwood stepped through the door. "Betsy and Tabby, I think, and maybe Luck? It's probably too late to save them. You really don't need to go out there." She looked worried, and he heard the fear underlying her words.

"I swear they won't hurt me," he said.

"I'm not worried they'll hurt you," she said. "I'm worried..." Her voice trailed off.

"Yes?"

"Nothin'," she said.

He moved past her. The dogs were barking on the other side of the creek now, heading for the river near where his property met up with the widow's land.

He gave chase, relying more on his familiarity with the land than his eyes. What stars were visible glowed softly through haze. The night air hung thick and stifling as ran along the edge of the cornfield. It had been a hot, wet summer, with storms almost daily. The creek, a bare trickle along a gravel bed when he'd settled the land, was now brown and roiling and several yards wide. Even in the dark, he knew where the rocks were just beneath the surface and with two jumps was across. He passed by the chicken coop, the door still open, feathers drifting in the air. He didn't stop to see if Zeeky was right about which hens were missing, but ran straight on into the forest, following the howls of the dogs.

He frowned as he realized how quickly he was catching up to the baying dogs. They were no longer giving chase. With luck, they'd treed the dragons. But, there was a second possibility. He pushed through the brambles that ran along the river bank until he reached the open spot where he and Jeremiah went fishing. He finally spotted the dogs, racing back and forth along the bank, barking with frustration at the river. The water churned too violently for the dogs to risk jumping in. Would the dragons have taken the risk?

"Damn it," Bitterwood said with a sigh, realizing how the tatterwings had gotten away. He moved up the bank to the old oak tree. The dugout canoe he kept there was gone.

He ran back to the water and splashed into it, the swift current nearly knocking him off his feet. Shin deep, he stared downriver, trying to make sense of the shadows. The tatterwings couldn't have gotten far even with the swiftness of the current. He thought perhaps he saw a faint movement in the darkness near the river bend a hundred yards away. He plucked an arrow from his quiver, took aim at a target that might have existed only in his imagination, and let the shot fly. In the dark, he could track the swift arrow only a few dozen feet before it vanished. He thought he heard a yelp, but he couldn't be sure over the roar of the water and the noise of the dogs.

He lowered his bow, feeling the stiffness of his body. Once, he'd lived for nights such as this, pursuing dragons through the darkness. In those years, he'd lived off the land, sleeping by day, often going weeks without cooked meals. He'd been lean and hungry, fueled by hatred, and certainly hadn't needed an excuse to hunt a dragon other than that it was a dragon.

But that was a different life. He slept in a bed now, and, though he worked hard all day, his once angular form was softening as he daily ate his fill of food grown from his own land. Though he had no help other than Zeeky and Jeremiah, and despite his lack of practice in working the land, his farm had been far more productive than any other in the area. Part of this was the richness of the soil by the river, and part of this was due to the rather unusual speed and strength of the creature to which he yoked his plow. Bitterwood had work to do in the morning. He couldn't be out all night chasing chicken thieves, and he might have been tempted to go back to bed if it wasn't for the canoe. It wasn't his; he'd borrowed it from the widow in the spring, before the garden was producing and fishing had been an important part of their diet. She hadn't had it in the water since her husband and eldest son died during the battle of Dragon Forge, and she'd told him he could use it as long as he wanted, but he couldn't stomach the thought of telling her that he'd let a couple of dragons get away with it. The more he thought of admitting any defeat by a dragon, however small, the more his guts felt full of broken glass, and with no further thought he knew he would chase these dragons to hell if needed.

His weariness left him as he dashed back through the woods toward the house, the dogs at his heels. He stopped when he spotted a small pale form wobbling through the underbrush a little ways off to his left. It was a hen, probably one the dragons had stolen then dropped in their haste to flee the dogs. He snatched it up and tucked it under his arm, carrying across the swollen creek to deposit it in the chicken coop once more. His eyes flickered quickly over the forms within.

"If you're counting," said Zeeky, emerging from the darkness beside him. "There's three missing, Bitsy, Tabby, and Luck, like I thought."

"I've got Tabby here," Bitterwood said, closing the door to the coop. "You shouldn't be out alone. Where's Jeremiah?"

"Still sleeping," she said. "And I'm not alone." She nodded toward the barn door, which was flung open. She made a chirping noise, and Skitter emerged from the barn, his copper scales glinting in the pale starlight.

Skitter was a long-wyrm, fifty feet long from snout to tail tip, sporting fourteen pairs of legs along his serpentine body. The long-wyrm could move twice as fast as any horse and if his stamina had limits, Bitterwood had yet to discover them. The beast was gentle and obedient as any of the dogs and the expense of keeping such a creature fed was more than offset by Skitter's unnatural speed at drawing a plow through even the rockiest of soil.

Bitterwood leapt bareback onto the beast.

"There's no reason to go after them," said Zeeky, grabbing his boot. "The other hens are probably dead already."

"They stole the widow's canoe," said Bitterwood.

Zeeky frowned, looking even more worried.

"Why don't you want me to chase them?" said Bitterwood. "I thought you liked the chickens."

"I love all our animals," Zeeky said. "Just not enough to avenge their deaths."

"There's no chance I'll get hurt."

She shook her head. "You haven't killed a dragon in months."

"You're worried I'm out of practice?"

"I'm worried... it's just that..." Her voice trailed off. She let go of his boot. "It's nothing. You're gonna do what you're gonna do."

"I always say the same thing about you," he said, digging his heels into Skitter's sides.

The beast shot off, tearing along the muddy path toward the river. The long-wyrm's claws made a slurpy, sucking sound as it raced through the muck. Fortunately, the dragons in the canoe wouldn't hear him over the sound of the churning water.

He doubted the dragons had gotten far in the canoe. The dugout was heavy, and while the weight lent it stability on the water, it also made it tricky to steer. He suspected they could be no more than a few hundred yards downstream by now.

Fortunately, as fast as Skitter was on land, he was equally swift in the water. The great beast plunged into the river, obeying Bitterwood's chirping commands. It swam along the surface, easily navigating through the churn. Bitterwood shivered. Compared to the warmth of the sultry summer night, the rain-fed river felt almost icy.

He was only in the water for a few minutes before he spotted the abandoned canoe on the far bank. Skitter climbed the bank beside the vessel.

Bitterwood jumped down into the mud and looked at the dugout. It was half full of water and he quickly saw why. His arrow had hit its unseen mark after all. The bow and quiver had been given to him by the woman who called herself the Goddess. Through some magic he didn't understand, the arrows grew in the living quiver as perfectly straight twigs with leaves for fletching, and fresh arrows replaced the old ones almost as swiftly as he plucked them. The tips were tiny black dots that could punch a clean hole through anything, even a cast iron skillet. His arrow had left a small hole below the waterline on the left side of the canoe.

But it hadn't been only the canoe he'd hit. He sniffed, catching a familiar scent. The water in the canoe carried the faintest trace of blood. Running his hand along the bottom, he found the reason for the blood as he picked up a single hind-claw of a sky-dragon, cleanly severed at the first knuckle. His arrow had passed through the dragon's talon on its way through the bottom of the boat.

Bitterwood studied the ground surrounding the canoe. There were a hundred clues telling him which way the dragons had fled. Talon marks in the mud, bent branches, stray chicken feathers. Following them wouldn't be difficult. Of course, he probably didn't need his skills as a tracker to find the tatterwings. He knew exactly where they were going. Ten miles outside of Dragon Forge, along the road to Richmond, a sizable band of earth-dragons had taken up residence in the village of Multon, once the closest human town to the foundries, though every last resident had been slaughtered not long after Ragnar and Burke had captured Dragon Forge.

Why Burke hadn't driven the dragons out of Multon was a mystery to Bitterwood. Perhaps he didn't see the danger the dragons posed, since they were leaderless. The new dragon-king, Hex, claimed he had no use for an army. He even denied being king, despite his fondness for issuing proclamations. The earth-dragons, no longer employed as soldiers, also had little success as raiders. Burke's guns had made the local militia more than equal to the roughest earth-dragon, so they generally stayed well clear of Dragon Forge. Burke had also trained a hundred or so men to serve as rangers, patrolling the farmlands on the south side of the river, or at least patrolling those farms willing to pay for security. Bitterwood had never agreed to the ranger's protection. He viewed men who needed to fight with guns with almost the same level of disdain he had toward dragons. Burke's guns were loud, smelly, and slow to reload. He could kill a dozen dragons with his bow, silently, swiftly, before an encampment of dragons would even know of his presence. It disgusted him to see Burke's rangers acting brave because of their weapons. To Bitterwood, the guns were all noise and flash, and the men who carried them would likely break and run if ever faced with a foe with even a small measure of courage.

Of course, courage was in short supply among the dragons after their route at Dragon Forge. They survived only because Hex had inherited the vast wealth of his family and provided the earth-dragons with stores of corn and wheat while encouraging them to try their hand at farming. Instead of planting the grain, the dragons used it to make cheap, eye-watering whisky, which they sold to humans at the foundry despite Burke's efforts to put an end to the trade. Bitterwood would likely find the tatterwings among the drinking houses in Multon. No winged dragon would keep company with a tatterwing, but earth-dragons didn't care who or what drank their whisky.

The hairs rose on Bitterwood's neck as he heard a rustling in the reeds behind him. He placed an arrow against his bowstring, preparing to aim toward the noise, then stayed his hand as a breeze carried the familiar scent of a hog.

"I see you found the canoe," said Zeeky, as she pushed through the tall reeds beside him. Bitterwood smirked as he saw her mount. She was riding Poocher, the hog that he was forbidden to eat. She'd rescued the pig when he was only a runt, and under her tender care the swine had grown to monstrous size. Unlike Skitter, the hog wouldn't pull a plow. Bitterwood was tired of people at the market asking how much he wanted for the pig. He spoke as little as possible with his fellow men. Explaining the pig's heroic backstory required more words than he normally chose to share.

"Pigs make better meats than they do mounts," Bitterwood said, giving her a sideways glance. "You're lucky you didn't drown crossing the river."

"Poocher's too fat to ever go under the water," said Zeeky. "He might not be as fast as Skitter, but he's got a better nose. Following y'all wasn't a problem."

"You didn't need to follow at all," said Bitterwood. Zeeky's fearlessness was both a quality he greatly admired and a trait he found exhausting.

"It's not like I could sleep with you out here," she said.

"Then you could have kept practicing your reading," he said. Not that he she needed the practice. When he'd met Zeeky, she couldn't read or write a single letter. But, early in the spring he'd carved a sign that read "no trespassing" to put up at the road. Once Zeeky realized he knew how to read and write, she pestered him to teach her. He'd given her a few basic lessons in ABC's and a few weeks later she'd gone into town and borrowed books from Burke. Now that it was summer, she was already racing through books filled with words he couldn't begin to puzzle out.

Zeeky smiled softly as she said, "Somebody had to come out here to make sure you didn't do nothing foolish."

Bitterwood frowned. Zeeky often spoke to him like she was the adult and he the child. She'd been headstrong and self-assured when he first met her as a runaway, already blessed with her talent for communicating with animals via the postures and eye motions and soft grunts that other people could never quite perceive. But ever since their trip to the underground realm of the Goddess, Zeeky had been getting smarter and acting older with each day. She'd told him that she'd learned the Goddess had changed her in the womb to give her special abilities. He was grateful for her gifts; she'd tamed the long-wyrm, and under her care the chickens laid more eggs and the cows produced more milk. If it weren't for her rather stubborn views about whether or not pigs should be eaten, she'd have been the perfect adopted daughter for any farmer.

Her eyes were fixed on his face. Suddenly, the truth struck him. She was reading him like she read her animals. She saw something inside him that worried her, something he might not even be aware of.

"What's the real reason you're here?" he asked.

"We've got the canoe," she said. "Let's go home."

"No," he said.

"Ain't no point in chasing those dragons," said Zeeky. "It's too late for those chickens."

"But we have more chickens," said Bitterwood. "So do our neighbors. A successful thief is a bold thief. Maybe you don't want to avenge a chicken. What would you be saying now if they'd killed your pig?"

"Poocher can take care of himself. And if you're worried about him, you could always let him sleep inside with me and the dogs."

Bitterwood sighed. This again.

"Let's go back," said Zeeky.

"You go back," said Bitterwood, feeling something inside him harden. It wasn't only the chickens at risk. Allowing the dragons to think that there would be no consequences put Zeeky and Jeremiah in danger as well. It was more than just the fact that a successful thief was a bold thief. It would be bad enough if the thieves were human. But dragons? Dragons had stolen the world from mankind. Only now had men finally taken some of it back. To let even one think he could steal from humans was unthinkable.

"Go home," said Bitterwood.

"Please don't go," she said.

"I'm telling you, I won't be in any danger!"

"You're already in danger," she said, sounding on the verge of tears. "It's just like the first time!"

"The first time?"

"In the barn. The night I found you."

He said nothing.

"You were kind to me," she said. "You were instantly a friend. And then you heard that the dragons were near and you changed."

"I—"

"You turned me over to the first person you could find and went off to kill dragons. You never did come back for me. It was pure luck we met again."

This was concise and accurate summary of events, he had to admit.

"And now we're a family," she said.

"Yes," said Bitterwood. "And, long ago, I lost one family to dragons. I won't do so again."

"You'll risk everything if you chase them," she said.

"It's just two thieves," he said.

"That's not what I'm scared of," she said. "I'm scared of you! You can't see it, but I can. There's two people inside your skin. There's the farmer and then there's... someone else. Someone cruel. Someone who knows nothing but hate and blood and death."

He looked down at the claw marks in the mud. He took a deep breath of the rich, wet air. He found the faint scent of the dragons, a musky, snaky odor. He closed his eyes, imagining them before him, imagining their fear as they realized who was chasing them this night. He wanted to hear them whimper in terror. He needed to see them dead.

Zeeky was right. This wasn't about the canoe or the chickens, about his neighbors or even his adopted children. It was about his hunger. His hatred of dragons hadn't disappeared when he became a farmer. It had just gone deeper into the shadows inside him, waiting patiently until it could feed once more. For now, the dragons and the humans in this little corner of the world lived in uneasy peace. In the day to day distractions of toiling on the land and providing food for his adoptive son and daughter, there were moments, hours even, when it felt as if his battle was over. He'd fought against dragons all alone, and now Burke and the rebels at the fort had taken up the cause, and he was doing the world no great harm by putting down his bow and taking up a plow and allowing others to fight his fight.

All these thoughts were quick to leap to the front of his mind, eager to rationalize why he deserved happiness and peace and family. But occasionally, usually in the evenings, in the deep shadows of the forests, or a dark corner of the barn, he could see the gray ghost of his hatred standing silently, watching coolly, and building strength. That ghost was out there now, somewhere along the trail, patiently waiting to command his body once more.

"Please," said Zeeky. "We got so much to do in the morning. Let's go get some sleep."

Bitterwood looked down at the bow in his hand, the best bow he'd ever used, and felt the quiver of ever-refreshed arrows upon his back, and wanted more than anything to make use of these priceless tools against his enemies. No. Not more than anything. As he looked at Zeeky's forlorn eyes, he knew there was something he wanted more. His own happiness meant little to him, but every smile he put on Zeeky's face was precious to him.

"Very well," he said. "Burke is always saying how he's the law in these parts now. I'll go talk to him tomorrow. See what he'll do about this."

"Good," said Zeeky, though there was still a note of worry in her voice. As Poocher waded back into the river, Bitterwood wanted to say something to comfort her, to assure her his days of chasing dragons in the darkness were behind him, but he couldn't find the words.

THE NEXT MORNING, once his chores were done, Bitterwood saddled up his horse and headed to town. He chose not to ride Skitter into Dragon Forge, partly because Skitter tended to spook other animals and partly because Bitterwood worried the gunmen at the fort might use Skitter for target practice. They tended to shoot at anything with scales, a policy he mostly agreed with.

The road along the river was bustling this morning. When Burke had taken over Dragon Forge, he'd been worried about how he was going to feed his army. He was drawing his rebels from farms, leaving few people to work the land. Fortunately, nature had smiled upon the rebellion. A wet winter had been followed by a sunny spring, the type of weather when even a walking stick leaning against a door might sprout roots. The old men, women, and children left upon the farms had more than enough food in their gardens, with abundance left to feed the soldiers. The land Bitterwood farmed had belonged to a man whose wife and children had died from yellow-mouth a few years back. Though still a young man, the bereaved farmer neglected his land, and when the rebellion came, he was eager to leave his fields behind.

Bitterwood had paid him well for the farm. During his years as a dragon slayer, he'd killed more than a few dragons carrying purses of gold. At the time, money meant little to him. He'd taken most of the coins he'd gained and left them quietly on doorsteps of small farms, but had also put aside modest caches of treasure here and there to purchase supplies he needed, such as the occasional horse. As fate would have it, he'd hidden quite a few stashes of coins near Dragon Forge, and had started his new life as a farmer in modest comfort.

He smelled the town long before he say the fortress walls. The foundries hadn't grown cold once since Burke took over, and the fog of coal smoke that hung over the town gave the surrounding land a somber gloom. Even the men along the walls were painted in this solemn pallet, their faces gray with soot, staring as he approached, reminiscent of the ghost of his former life that sometimes stared at him from the shadows.

Bitterwood rode through the wide open gates without being stopped by the guards, which irked him. Not even half a year since the rebellion and already the guards seemed more bored than vigilant. Few people truly feared another attempt by the dragons to reclaim the fort. Hex no longer funded an army, and none of the numerous factions of the sun-dragons had yet gained enough power to organize a fresh campaign to crush the rebellion.

Bitterwood had imagined that a world without dragons would be paradise, but Dragon Forge looked, smelled, and sounded like hell. The ever-present smoke stank of rotten eggs and the streets reeked of piss. The walls constrained the city so that over the centuries buildings had been built atop buildings, giving the place a cramped, claustrophobic air, and made navigating the narrow alleys akin to finding one's way through a maze. It was nearly noon and people still slept in the alleys next to ramshackle saloons, sleeping off the previous night's drunkenness. Or, perhaps, the morning's drunkenness, given the number of men he saw stumbling woozily along the plank sidewalks.

He arrived at the center of the town square, one of the few open spaces with a view of the sky, but the openness provided no relief from the oppression of the city. Seven men hung from gallows in the center of the square, their bodies twisting slowly in the breeze. The age of dragons killing men drew towards its end, so now mankind would have to step in to fill their own graves.

Bitterwood dismounted in front of the foundry office that Burke had turned into a makeshift town hall. As he approached, the two guards by the door stepped into his path.

"I'm here to see Burke," said Bitterwood.

"Burke's busy," said one of the guards, a runty kid with bad skin.

"He may pass," said a voice from above. Bitterwood looked up and saw Anza, Burke's daughter, at the window above the door.

The guards nodded and stepped aside.

Bitterwood went into the foundry office, then up the stairs into the huge attic where Burke did most of his tinkering. In contrast with the squalor outside, the attic was meticulous, the floors gleaming with polish. The scent of pine soap alleviated the foul coal stench of the foundry.

Burke was seated at a desk, bent over jagged shards of black iron, studying them with a magnifying glass. Anza stood beside him, her arms crossed, her eyes locked on Bitterwood.

Without looking up, Burke said, "What brings you to town, Bant?"

"Dragons," said Bitterwood. "A trio of tatterwings stole some of my chickens last night."

Burke looked up from the magnifying glass. "All the more reason you should let my rangers guard your farm."

"What good does it do me to have a band of men trampling through my crops once or twice a night as part of their patrol?" asked Bitterwood. "You think dragons don't have eyes? They'll just sneak in once your rangers have moved on."

"Then what do you want me to do about it?" asked Burke.

"You've got men hanging from gallows. Why not thieving dragons?"

"Because dragons aren't dumb enough to come into the fort to steal, rape, and kill."

"Then go out of the fort. You know they've taken over Multon. You've got an army. Use it."

Burke leaned back in his chair, rubbing his eyes. "For now, Multon is outside the defensible perimeter. We could take the town, but I don't know that we could hold it. There's too much ground between here and there for us to defend supply lines to any size force that would make a difference. Mankind once ruled this world, Bant. I intend that we do so again. But, we need to be realistic. We have constraints on our manpower and resources. The surest way to see that our rebellion fails is to push too far, too fast."

"With Ragnar gone, you've gotten timid," said Bitterwood.

"With Ragnar gone, I can finally make rational choices," said Burke. "Ragnar would have already sent out armies to try to liberate other towns."

"And what's stopping you? There are men throughout the kingdom who'd turn into soldiers willingly enough if you put one of your guns in their hands. You can make all the guns you need now that you control Dragon Forge," said Bitterwood.

Burke motioned to the pile of metal shards. "Guns that still have a bad habit of exploding." He shook his head. "Guns in the hands of men who are even more explosive. Those men I hung this morning? All murderers. I built these weapons to kill dragons, but should have known they'd be turned against fellow men quickly enough."

"It doesn't help that your men are drunk all the time," said Bitterwood.

"I can't argue with that," said Burke, with a heavy sigh. "But there's a fine balance here. A lot of the rebels view whiskey as a vital part of compensation. If I were to ban alcohol outright, a quarter of my army would abandon me. Maybe more. Don't forget I used to run a tavern. There's nothing inherently wrong with men having a few drinks. It's a minority of men who abuse the privilege."

"Your men are drinking because they're bored," said Bitterwood. "Sending them out to kill every last dragon in Multon would sober them up."

"That seems like an overreaction to the theft of a few chickens," said Anza, sounding amused.

"Worse, I'm sure it's exactly what the dragons want," said Burke.

"They want to be wiped out?"

Burke shook his head. "The sky-dragons at the College of Spires are still trying desperately to get their hands on one of our guns to find out how it works. Our spies have seen sky-dragons flying in and out of Multon. If we were to attack in force, a dragon escaping with a single captured shotgun could destroy our advantage in arms. It nearly happened once already. Anza was almost killed breaking into the College of Spires to recover the weapon."

"Almost killed is the same as saying I wasn't killed," said Anza. "I could do it again."

Burke shook his head. "Bant, since you won't pay to have my rangers protect your land, I'll do it for free. They're already patrolling your neighbors, so it's not difficult to add you to the patrol. That's really all I can do."

"That's all you're willing to do," said Bitterwood.

"My father tells me you were once a fearsome dragon-slayer," said Anza. "Why should you even need our help dealing with a few tatterwings?"

"I've been asking myself that all morning," said Bitterwood.

BITTERWOOD RODE HOME in a sour mood. What had he expected from Burke? Long ago, the two of them had fought shoulder to shoulder against the dragons in an earlier rebellion in Conyers. After that rebellion had been crushed by the sun-dragons, Burke had gone into hiding while Bitterwood alone of all the rebels had continued to fight, living in the darkness, hunting dragons while his fellow men slept soundly, their dreams seemingly untroubled by the dragons' oppression. Burke's cautious, cool-headed approach to this war against the dragons would never bring him victory. Bitterwood wasn't even certain Burke was still fighting a war. He seemed content ruling this tiny patch of earth and leaving the rest of the world to the dragons.

"Isn't this precisely what you've done?" Bitterwood looked over his shoulder, even though he knew the voice that asked this was his own, and existed only in his mind. "You've put down your bow and taken up a plow," the voice continued. "How is this not surrender?"

"It's different now," said Bitterwood, aloud. "The children must be fed."

"Give them to others," said the silent voice. "You owe them nothing."

"I owe the dragons even less!" Bitterwood said, on the verge of shouting. "Why should the damned lizards be my responsibility alone? Why must I sacrifice body and soul while my fellow men do next to nothing? Am I to surrender everything, my home and my happiness?"

"Hatred is your home and happiness," said the ghost within him.

Bitterwood clenched his jaw, aware of the madness of arguing with himself, especially out loud. But the ghost was wrong. His hatred wasn't his happiness. Hearing Zeeky talk to the cows as she milked them each morning, that was happiness. Seeing Jeremiah smile as he pulled up a fish trap to discover a fat catfish. That made him content. Watching his crops grow, seeing tomatoes fat and red on the vine, the rows of corn growing taller than himself, these things gave him peace and comfort and hope.

"The truth is in your dreams," his ghost whispered.

Bitterwood could not argue with this. In his dreams, he often saw wounded dragons crawling through mud, whimpering for mercy, their bodies riddled with arrows. There was blood in these dreams, the smell of bile and excrement, and cries of terror. To any other man, his dreams were nightmares. But from such dreams, Bitterwood would wake up laughing.

A WEEK PASSED and the missing chickens were mostly forgotten. The hole in the canoe had been patched and he'd returned it to the widow so he wouldn't have to feel responsible for it any more. The happiness he'd contemplated on his ride back from Dragon Forge seemed real to him again. Perhaps bringing life out of his little patch of land with his adopted children was all he needed in this world. Yet, every time he found himself on the verge of joy, he thought of how, long ago, he'd felt this joy before, with his wife Recanna, and their children, and the peach orchards surrounding their village, and how the dragons had taken away all he had loved. Could he endure such pain again?

It was almost with a sense of relief, then, that he greeted the three horsemen who came riding down the dirt path to his farm one afternoon. They wore green cloaks and glinting steel badges, and had shotguns cradled in their arms as they rode. These were some of Burke's rangers, responsible for enforcing—what had been his phrasing?—the defensible perimeter. In exchange for their protection, all the farmers were supposed to feed the rangers and provide shelter as needed plus pay a small fee each month. All this was on top of a tax levied each market day. Bitterwood knew that men couldn't fight on empty bellies, and understood Burke's men must be paid. Still, one reason the humans had finally rebelled against their dragon overlords was that the dragon armies had always viewed men's property as their own. The thought that Burke had the same view toward the products of his labor was distasteful.

Zeeky came up from the barn as the rangers approached, the dogs barking and dancing around her. Jeremiah watched from the door of the cabin as the men drew nearer, halting their horses before Bitterwood.

"You must be Bant," the lead horseman said without dismounting. He was a young man, with a thin but wiry build, his face and fists sporting numerous scars. "I'm Priter. This here's Bo and that's Wessing," he said, nodding to his two companions. They also had scarred faces showing they were no strangers to violence, though Wessing looked older than Bitterwood and had a drooped, weary appearance that gave the impression he was more eager for a nap than a fight.

"Burke sent you round to guard my farm," said Bitterwood.

"Said dragons stole some of your chickens," said Priter. "You're not the only farm they've hit of late. Guess they must be running low on food over in Multon."

"Or maybe you rangers aren't very good at your job," said Bitterwood.

"Bo, show him the sack," said Priter.

Bo was the biggest of the three rangers, with an unkempt beard, and his eyes hidden beneath the brim of a large leather hat. He loosened a sack that hung from his saddle and emptied the contents. The severed head of a sky dragon rolled in the dust at Bitterwood's feet, its pale blue scales glinting in the sun.

Zeeky gasped, placing her hands over her mouth. The dogs rushed forward to sniff the bloodied head, which smelled ripe in the heat of the day.

"We caught him in the woods near the widow's place," said Priter.

"Was he stealing chickens?" asked Zeeky.

"It's not like we caught him with a chicken in his mouth, but he was a tatterwing. He couldn't have been up to any good."

Bitterwood nodded. "That's one down. Just uncounted thousands to go."

Priter chuckled. "Well, I can't be responsible for those uncounted thousands. But, I can guard your farm, assuming you're finally ready to pay up."

"Burke said you'd watch the place for free."

"Sure," said Priter. "But we have a lot of farms on our patrol. It's customary for those who want us to spend a little extra time on their land to chip in a little more. It doesn't have to be gold. Dobbs down the road pays with a jug of blackberry wine once a week. The Darnagins give us chickens."

"The whole point in wanting you around is not to lose any more chickens," said Bitterwood.

"The dragons know they've stolen from you once and gotten away," said Priter. "What if next time they take more than chickens? I've seen you ride into town on a fine-looking horse. Earth-dragons love horsemeat a lot more than chickens."

"They like hogs even more," said Bo, eying Poocher's enormous form in the pen beside the barn. "Lord Almighty, that's a big 'un."

"Earth-dragons ain't bothered us," said Zeeky. "Just some mangy old tatterwings, and they're too pathetic to go after something as big as a horse or a pig."

"Then you're lucky," said Priter. "From what we've heard, further up the Forge Road the earth-dragons are eating up pretty much anything in sight. They mostly stay clear of this side of the river because they've seen what these can do." He patted the gun barrel. "But food's starting to get scarce over there, since no humans are left on that side of the river to grow crops. That's why the tatterwings are taking chances. Only a matter of time before the earth-dragons follow. Be a shame to lose a horse because you're too cheap to guarantee yourself a little extra attention."

Bitterwood said, "And once everyone starts paying, you're back to the same place you started. Too few people watching too many farms. So you jack up the price. I'm not an idiot, boy."

"Then you're smart enough to see why you need us," said Priter.

"I'm smart enough to see you're taking a job that needs to be done and using it to line your pockets. Does Burke know about your extortion?"

"We're not extorting you," said Priter. "Just the opposite. We're offering protection."

"From the dragons? Or from you?" said Zeeky, giving the men a sour look.

Bitterwood, despite his hostility to the men, had until this moment still considered letting them patrol his land. But, he trusted Zeeky's instincts, and if the girl didn't like these men, that was a good enough reason for him to send them away.

He knelt and picked up the sky-dragon's head. He tossed it back to Bo, who caught it awkwardly. The dogs raced around his horse, barking, and the horse pranced around skittishly.

"I think we'll be okay without you," said Bitterwood. "Be on your way."

"Don't come crying to us when the dragons hit you again," said Priter, scowling.

The men turned their horses back to the dirt path and galloped off, the dogs barking after them.

"Nut!" yelled Zeeky. "Catfish! Behave!"

At her words, the two dogs broke off from their chase, loping back with looks on their faces that resembled grins.

Jeremiah walked over and rested his arms on the fence. "Maybe we should have paid 'em."

"What could those fools do?" Zeeky said, scornfully. "No dragons can sneak onto the farm without me or the dogs catching on. And even if a whole army of dragons came across the river, I'd just have to let Skitter out of the barn to send 'em flyin'."

Bitterwood noted that, in Zeeky's plan, he played no role at all in defending the farm. To her, his former life as a killer was just that, a former life, and he need not kill in her name. He felt something stir in him, pride perhaps, or simple hope, that he might yet be good enough to be a father for these orphaned children.

"You will never be happy." said the familiar voice that haunted him, so loud he half expected the children to hear it. "The dragons are still out there. And I'm still in here."

"IT'S MARKET DAY!" Zeeky said, throwing off her covers at the first cock crow.

Bitterwood rose stiffly as Jeremiah and the dogs continued to slumber.

"Wake up, sleepy heads!" she said, and the dogs lifted their heads, their eyes drooping and bleary. "You too!" she said, shaking Jeremiah. The boy grumbled incoherent syllables as he pulled his pillow over his head.

From beneath the pillow, his muffled voice whined, "I don't see why I have to go."

"We all have to go," said Zeeky, lighting the fire in the woodstove.

Bitterwood pulled the pillow away from Jeremiah. "One day, you'll own this farm. You need to learn how to haggle."

"Why won't I own this farm?" asked Zeeky.

"Well, hopefully, you'll get married," said Bitterwood.

Zeeky stuck her tongue out. "No way." Zeeky was still young enough not to show any fascination with boys, though Bitterwood didn't know how much longer that would last. Neither Jeremiah or Zeeky knew their exact ages. Calendars hadn't been a thing in Big Lick, where time was measured mainly in seasons. Bitterwood guessed she was about ten, and Jeremiah maybe twelve. Both were thin as saplings with fine hair blonde as corn silk. Both had spent their early years in a remote mountain village where they seldom saw strangers. Their reactions to market day couldn't be more different. Zeeky loved the crowds, the bustle and noise, and would talk effusively with anyone who so much as offered her a hello, and even strike up one sided conversations with the stray dogs and cats that infested the streets of the town. Jeremiah, on the other hand, seemed to pull even deeper inside himself among the crowds, with a shyness and fear of others that left Bitterwood aching. He'd thought himself the ultimate loner, living like a ghost for twenty years. He'd perfected the art of not being noticed, and never stayed in one place long enough for anyone to care who he might be. He knew loneliness in a way few other men ever could, and hated to see Jeremiah sealing himself off in his own solitude. Of course, the first time Jeremiah had been to Dragon Forge, he'd been bullied by older boys and one of the foundry men had even tried to kill him when they learned he carried the disease of yellow-mouth. Still, bad memories or no, Jeremiah would have to learn to fend for himself among his fellow men. He wouldn't learn to deal with others by hiding all the time on the farm.

After breakfast, they hitched up the horse to the cart and walked beside it into town. The cart groaned beneath the weight of corn, cabbages, and cucumbers, tomatoes, sweet potatoes, and bushels of tart blackberries plucked from the vines along the river. Zeeky had to tell the dogs three times to stop following; a rare instance of them not obeying instantly, probably because Zeeky secretly wanted the dogs to come along. But the last thing Bitterwood needed was for his dogs to get into fights with the strays in town, or, worse, to wag their tails and find the company of another dog pleasant enough that Zeeky would insist that they not leave the dogs' new friend behind.

The fort stank as badly as ever with the foundry belching smoke, but on market day the town took on a different atmosphere. Under the rows of pole barns that formed the market, his hunger was stirred by the scent of tomatoes fresh off the vine, corn still warm from the sun, and the sweet perfume of blackberries ripe to the threshold of fermentation. Grills were set up throughout the market where you could buy roasted corn slathered in fresh butter, griddled cakes sticky with berry syrup, and skewers of pork grilled before booths overflowing with smoked hams and sausages. Fortunately, Zeeky never insisted on bringing Poocher here. Not that Bitterwood worried that the pig might be disturbed by the sight of all his butchered brethren. He had already accepted that he'd never get to eat Poocher. Finding out exactly how much money the people at the market would offer for the pig was something he'd just as soon not know.

They'd arrived early, before the city got too hot, and the energy in the market was lively, almost festive. Bitterwood asked fair prices for his goods and for the most part got them. He was happy that Jeremiah seemed to be paying attention to the niceties of the commerce, and the boy didn't grumble too much when he had to help a buyer load bushels of corn onto his cart. Zeeky, on the other hand, paid no attention at all to the buying and selling of vegetables and instead took up a conversation with a woman two spaces down and kept the conversation going most of the morning. Bitterwood almost called her back, worried that she might be bothering the woman, but whenever he glanced their way the woman seemed to be enjoying the conversation as much as Zeeky. Besides, it was good for the girl to get her talking done here. Neither Bitterwood nor Jeremiah could hold up their end of a long conversation with her. Honestly, she probably got more words out of Poocher. The way that pig grunted and squealed in answer to her words was very much like a conversation, and he wouldn't have been shocked if one day he'd gone into pen and found the pig capable of intelligible speech.

By noon, their produce had been turned into a heavy sack of coins, and a portion of these coins had been turned into cornmeal, flower, lard, salt, and a few pieces of hard candy for Zeeky and Jeremiah, plus a bucket of nails and a new saw. They left town just in time, Bitterwood felt, as some of the farmers took their coins to the rows of saloons tucked into the alleys and already several men staggered drunkenly through the streets.

Jeremiah studied the stumbling men. "Are they ill?" he asked, sounding worried. Having survived yellow-mouth, the boy flinched at any sign of disease in his fellow men.

"They're only drunk," said Bitterwood. "Let's be on our way."

For the journey home, they could ride. Jeremiah crawled into the back of the cart and instantly fell asleep. Bitterwood sat next to Zeeky, who told the horse to head home. The horse snorted and obeyed.

"Maybe I should be a teacher," Zeeky announced.

"What put that idea into your head?"

"The woman I was talking to. Bethann. She can't read."

"Most people can't."

"But it's so easy!" said Zeeky.

"Jeremiah doesn't think so," said Bitterwood. "I didn't think so, either, when I first learned."

"Who taught you?"

Bitterwood frowned. He hadn't thought about Hezekiah, the false prophet, in a long time.

"A stranger," said Bitterwood. "A stranger who came to my village."

A stranger who had killed his brother, and uncle, and a dozen other men, all in the name of a God who existed only in a book. He'd never told Zeeky any of this. Never told her he once had his own daughters, never spoke about the wife he'd once loved. She had her own burdens. His past would forever haunt him, but he saw no need that she ever know this pains. Those days of grief were long ago, he told himself. He was a man of the earth now, a man who lived in the here and now, beneath the sun, rooted in soil, washed in rain, alive once more, no longer a prisoner of his memories, no longer a slave of the dead.

"But I'm not dead," said the voice within him.

"I never said you were," said Zeeky, looking confused. "What an odd thing to say."

The realization he'd said the words out loud made him clench his jaw tightly. It was only the heat of the day that had made his tongue speak without him willing it. The ghost of his old life had no real power over him, did it?

BITTERWOOD REALIZED the significance of the buzzards before Zeeky. She saw them, no doubt, since she saw everything, but she probably didn't have his ability to map out on the land the spot above which the airborne beasts flew, a skill he'd perfected hunting sky-dragons. His blood grew cold. The buzzards circled above his house.

They rode on a little further. The house still couldn't be seen beyond the trees and tall brush on each side of the road.

Bitterwood put his hand on Zeeky's hand and said, "Stop the horse."

She nodded, made a soft whinny noise, and the horse stopped.

"What's wrong?" she asked. "Are the buzzards—?"

"Wait here," he said. "Unhitch the horse and wake your brother. Be ready to ride back to town if I say so."

"Do you think it's dragons?" she said, looking uncertain as she said it.

Bitterwood understood her confusion. She'd heard the gossip at the market about other farms being raided by dragons, but, so far, the raids always came at night. Unfortunately, tatterwings weren't stupid. If they knew about the market day, they also knew which farms would be mostly abandoned.

"It's probably nothing," said Jeremiah, sitting up, rubbing his eyes, glancing at the buzzards. "One of the dogs killed a rabbit, maybe."

"Probably nothing," said Bitterwood, nodding.

"It wouldn't be nothing to the poor rabbit," said Zeeky.

"Just get the horse ready and stay alert," said Bitterwood. Without looking back, he leapt the ditch by the road and pushed through the brush into the woods. He moved swiftly and silently through the shade until he emerged at the edge of his cornfield. He crept cautiously through the rows crouching when he caught sight of the house.

Everything was silent, which was the worst thing he could possibly hear. With the wind coming from the west, the dogs should have caught scent of him by now and come out barking to greet him.

He emerged from the corn, alert to any movement. His heart sank when he saw the dogs. Both Nut and Catfish were dead, hacked crudely with something sharp and heavy, most likely a battle-axe. He moved closer, looking for footprints. Unfortunately, the rains of the previous week had given way to several days of heat that had left the hard packed ground around his cabin too firm for even the heavy foot of an earth-dragon to leave marks. He suspected that it must have been an earth-dragon and not a tatterwing that killed the dogs. The battle-axe was a favored weapon of earth-dragons. Tatterwings would have used spears.

On the other hand, earth-dragons weren't particularly picky about what meat they ate. They would hardly leave behind two well-muscled hounds, unless they had a bigger feast in mind.

Bitterwood's heart was heavy as he moved to the pen next to the barn. Poocher was gone. There was blood everywhere, and evidence of where the hog's body had been dragged from the pen. Here, in the muck, the claw prints of earth-dragons were abundant. At least three of them. To remove the carcass, they'd used a cart drawn by an ox-dog from the looks of it. Curious. To attack in plain daylight was one thing. Moving the carcass via cart meant they had to follow the road, not toward town, obviously, but upriver two miles to the next bridge, which was guarded by rangers. Of course, the river wasn't as swollen as it had been even a week ago. There were two or three places where the river might be forded. Or perhaps the earth-dragons were even hungrier than he thought and gambling that they could overpower the rangers at the bridge.

Bitterwood frowned at the possibility that the earth-dragons might already be dead, shot down by the rangers. Losing Poocher... this was going to kill Zeeky. She'd endured a great deal of tragedy over the last year, and through it all the pig had been by her side, a faithful companion, more loyal to her than any dog. If Poocher's killers died at the guns of the rangers it would be a very hollow justice.

He moved to the barn door and swung it open. Skitter was still inside, sleeping soundly. The beast had been created by the Goddess to dwell in caves. While it obediently pulled a plow in daylight, it preferred to sleep during the day. Bitterwood wasn't surprised the earth-dragons had steered clear of the barn. Skitter gave off an odor that made any animals nervous. Not that humans particularly liked the smell either.

Assured that his transportation was safe, Bitterwood returned to the cabin to find his bow. He stopped short when he saw Jeremiah on the horse in the yard, looking pale as he stared at Bitterwood.

"I told you to stay... where's Zeeky?" Bitterwood asked.

"I told her were weren't supposed to come," said Jeremiah, weakly.

Bitterwood looked at the door of the cabin, which stood open. Zeeky emerged from the darkness inside, her cheeks wet with tears. In one hand, she carried his bow and in the other, his quiver.

"You were right," she said, her voice trembling. "You said... you said that the dragons would... and Poocher. He's... and the dogs... those poor dogs. I never thought... I never thought they'd hurt the dogs."

"They'll never hurt anything else," said Bitterwood, taking the bow. "The two of you go to the widow's house. Make sure she's okay. If any rangers come around, tell them what you know."

"Where are you going?" asked Jeremiah.

"You know where he's going," said Zeeky.

THE VILLAGE OF MULTON was only ten miles from Dragon Forge. Once it had housed two hundred humans working the fertile rolling hills but the fields now lay fallow. Every last man, woman, and child of the village had been slaughtered by earth-dragons in the aftermath of the first battle of Dragon Forge. When the dragon armies had been repulsed a second time by the rebels, a regiment of earth-dragons had set up camp among the abandoned structures. They remained there still, waiting for some winged dragon to come along and tell them what to do. Until then, they fed themselves by slaughtering every living thing within a few miles of the village, and occasionally their own brethren. Idle earth-dragons not under the command of a winged dragon would often argue among themselves, and these arguments were often settled by blows from a battle-axe, with the dragon walking away from such an encounter being deemed the winner of the debate, and the loser deemed dinner. And while earth-dragons weren't known for their mastery of fine culinary arts, they did possess a certain raw talent for fermentation and distillation. The seed corn and barley found in barns had been turned into whiskey and beer, the cabbages planted the previous season by humans had been turned into goom, and any fruit or wild berry in the area was well on its way to being wine.

Where there was booze there were buyers. Bitterwood watched the village from the upper branches of a tree, peeking through the leaves. His guts churned with bile as he watched a string of humans walk into the village then out again. He recognized some of the men from that morning's market. Going in, they carried chickens, wheelbarrows of cabbage and potatoes, loads of dried fish, and full purses. Coming out, they carried jugs and carted barrels. The fact that men would do willing commerce with creatures who had slaughtered their brothers disgusted Bitterwood beyond all words. Why hadn't Burke put an end to this trade?

His hatred built as he watched the life of Multon lazily unfold as the long summer evening wore on. Skitter was hidden in a nearby pond with only his nostrils peeking above the water. With a whistle, the beast would come to him, racing across the landscape in a copper colored blur. As tempting as it was to charge his death-wyrm right through the center of town and place arrows into the eye-sockets of any dragon who turned to see what the commotion about, Bitterwood knew he should wait for nightfall. His burning hatred of dragons had always been tempered by a cold, methodical approach to his vengeance. He'd killed more dragons than he could count, though he supposed the number must be in the thousands. As much as he found satisfaction in seeing fear in a dragon's eyes, most of these dead dragons had never even seen him before they died. He owed his survival through long years of bloodshed to stealth, cunning, and patience.

Not that his patience was being rewarded this afternoon. He'd spotted several carts drawn by ox-dogs, though none carried Poocher's carcass. He hadn't been able to track the cart once it reached the road, since there were too many wheel imprints to untangle due to it being a market day. He'd ridden upriver without finding clear evidence of where the dragons might have crossed, and found the bridge still guarded with no sign that the rangers there had seen action. It was vaguely plausible that he'd reached Multon before the earth-dragons thanks to Skitter's speed. Still, while ox-dogs weren't fast, they should have made it to Multon by now.

If they'd arrived before him, butchering a hog the size of Poocher would have been a time-consuming affair, likely carried out in open air. He hadn't seen any signs of a pig being butchered, but he had spotted a limping tatterwing with a bandaged hind-talon, moving through the streets with two fellow tatterwings, all three carrying jugs of whisky. On a gut level, Bitterwood felt certain these were the chicken thieves. There were other tatterwings moving about the town, but he didn't see any others with bandaged wounds.

Even though the tatterwings hadn't killed Poocher, he imagined they might know which of the earth-dragons had done the deed. To Bitterwood, the sequence of events was obvious. They'd returned to the village with their stolen chickens and mentioned to some earth-dragon that the bounty had come from a farm that housed the biggest hog they'd ever laid eyes on. After that, the earth-dragons likely couldn't have resisted the temptation. Which meant that none of this would have happened if he'd followed his impulse and tracked down the chicken thieves the first night. Zeeky had to be thinking the same thing. She might even feel responsible for Poocher's death. The thought of the sweet child bearing such a burden felt like a hand closing around his heart.

At last, the night arrived. In the dark, he guided Skitter behind a large barn near the edge of town and rode the beast onto the roof, since the long-wyrm could climb a vertical surface as easily as it moved over flat ground. No animals within the barn cried in alarm at Skitter's scent. Any horses or cows would have been eaten by the dragons long ago, and ox-dogs weren't traditionally housed in barns.

Not far away was the tavern at the center of town, once run by humans, now a central location for the dragons to sell their wares. The place was bustling with both dragons and men, and the grunting chants that passed for earth-dragon songs. He heard the laughter of human women though he hadn't seen any women come or go from the town. Probably whores, living permanently at the tavern.

Tomorrow, they'd need to find a new home. The place was well lit with lanterns, flames dancing within chimney glass above tin reservoirs filled with oil. The windows of the tavern were wide open to let in the cool night breeze. The task before him was no challenge. He'd downed dragons with an arrow to the eye in worse light and at twice the distance.

There was no reaction at all to his first arrows, which punctured the oil reservoirs of four of the lanterns, three near the window, and one on the far side of the room which he targeted just because it was the only one that was even slightly difficult. He waited a few seconds and heard a few of the chanting voices die off. Murmurs of confusion spread across the room as oil streamed down from the punctured lanterns. Satisfied the oil had enough time to drain, he followed up with arrows that shattered the chimneys. Women screamed, startled by the crash and rain of glass. The singing stopped entirely.

He let four more arrows fly. This time he targeted the handles and hooks from which the lanterns dangled. The three nearest the windows fell and instantly flames erupted through the room. The screams of the women were drowned out by the shrieks of earth-dragons realizing they were on fire. The last flame on the far side of the room continued to dance around its wick. He'd missed! Not that he now needed that lantern to help spread panic and flame, but, just to feel the job was done right, he released a fifth arrow, smiling as the flame dropped down into the pool of oil beneath it.

Every window and crack in the wall of the saloon now glowed with bright light. The flames from the oil found plentiful fuel in the ancient furniture, and overturned jugs of whiskey erupted in bright blue gouts of light and heat.

Everyone inside the tavern made a concerted effort to be outside the tavern all at once. There were shouts and curses and shrieks, as earth-dragons trampled over the men and women in their paths. Only a single earth-dragon stayed behind, beating at the flames with a thick rug. Bitterwood put an arrow through his heart. It wouldn't do to have the flames extinguished too quickly.

Bitterwood narrowed his eyes as he watched the door. The chaos of shapes spilling out into the street was half obscured with trailing smoke, and it was hard to tell in the flickering light which of the several tatterwings among the crowd were the ones he was looking for.

Then, he spotted one limping, and made out the bandaged talon as it hurried toward the barn where Bitterwood hid. He'd seen them come and go from the barn a few times, and guessed they likely lived here. With the noise and panic at the saloon, he'd have time to question these tatterwings without interference no matter how loud they screamed.

As he waited for the tatterwings to reach him, he heard one of the larger earth-dragons barking out orders. Suddenly a bucket brigade formed. Earth-dragons were clumsy and dim-witted as a rule, but once guided in a task by a strong leader their boundless strength and stamina could turn them into a formidable muscle powered machine. So far, he didn't know if anyone had even seen his arrows. The dragons couldn't know if this was an attack or some strange accident that had caused the lanterns to shatter spontaneously. While he saw advantages in allowing the dragons to continue their work in ignorance, there was something missing. There was panic and commotion, yes, but not terror. The dragons were afraid of losing the tavern, not of losing their lives.

He rose, confident his dark cloak concealed him from eyes dazzled by flames, and unleashed arrow after arrow. The bucket brigade dragons had been so thoughtful in lining up for him, one by one, like a row of bottles upon a fence one might use for target practice.

He didn't go for instant kills. An arrow through the gut would bring days of agony before death. An arrow in the throat would allow for several horrific moments of awareness as a dragon died, drowning in his own blood. And an arrow in the shoulder or thigh would bring pain, but leave the dragon conscious and aware and able to shout the one word he wanted to hear.

Five of the bucket brigade dragons fell. One still standing tore out the arrow jutting from his shoulder and stared at it, uncomprehending for long seconds before he cried, "Bitterwood!"

Once the word was spoken, it spread faster than the fire. "Bitterwood! Bitterwood!" The remnants of the bucket brigade fled for the cover of any house or shed they could find and in seconds the streets were cleared.

"Bitterwood?" said the limping dragon below as he reached the barn door. He stood while the door was opened by one of his companions. "Bitterwood's dead! He died when he assassinated Shandrazel. He struck the king with a poisoned dagger, but the king with his dying strength gutted the man."

"How do you gut a ghost?" one of his companions asked as he closed the door, sounding panicked. "Bitterwood's an evil spirit! The Ghost Who Kills, not a flesh and blood man!"

"Don't be a superstitious fool," the other companion grumbled. "Humans might believe in spirits, but we're above such things. The king didn't kill Bitterwood because there never was a Bitterwood. He's a myth, a legend!"

"A myth is even harder to gut than a ghost," the fearful dragon said.

"It's merely idiot earth-dragons panicking," said the cool-headed companion. "Someone knocked over a lantern and now everyone's acting like it's the end of the world."

Apparently, they hadn't seen any of his arrows, which made sense, since they'd been running away from the dragons he'd targeted.

"What's that smell?" said the tatterwing with the bandaged talon. Bitterwood suspected they'd caught Skitter's unique aroma.

"I smell it too," said the tatterwing who believed in ghosts. "It's like nothing I've ever smelled before. It's... unnatural. Evil."

The rational tatterwing sighed. "It's plainly something in the smoke. Goom smells evil enough when you drink it. I can only imagine how it must reek when it burns."

By now, Bitterwood had silently climbed down into the hayloft and crouched above the three dragons. The barn was darker than the surrounding night, lit only by the distant flames, the light flickering through the cracks in the barn and casting sinister shadows.

"Let's leave," said the superstitious companion.

"And go where?" asked the rational one.

"Richmond," said the wounded tatterwing. "I've heard rumors that most of the humans there have been killed and even a tatterwing can find easy pickings in the stuff they've left behind. But, I'll never walk that far. We'll need to steal an ox-dog and a cart."

"An excellent suggestion," said the rational tatterwing. "Ever since the rangers killed Nizel for cheating on the deal, I've been feeling that our days here are numbered."

"Those bastards," the wounded one growled. "We were idiots to ever trust humans. Though, you know, Nizel had it coming."

"True," said rational.

"True," said superstitious.

"True," said Bitterwood, in the darkness above them.

All three of the dragons grew quiet. In unison, slowly, slowly, they lifted their eyes toward him. From the unfixed qualities of their gazes, he could tell they couldn't see him. With his dark cloak, hunched over in the shadows, he blended into the bales of hay scattered around the loft.

"Who... who's there?" asked rational, swallowing hard.

"Truth," said Bitterwood.

Now their eyes fixed on him as he rose to stand on the edge of the loft, looking down into their fearful faces.

"Truth is what you fear most, after all," said Bitterwood, his voice gravelly and cold. "None of you became tatterwings because of your honest natures. You're thieves and traitors, the shame of your race, condemned by your brethren to fates worse than death. They've stolen the sky from you. Your fate at my hands will seem like mercy."

The rational one broke first, spinning around. But instead of fleeing the barn he ran into a stall and grabbed a spear leaning against the wall. Bitterwood recognized the spear as the kind used by the aerial guard. Rational likely had some training.

"I don't fear you, human!" the tatterwing snarled.

Bitterwood could have dropped him easily with his bow. Instead he leapt from the hayloft, knife in hand, rolling across the floor as he landed. He sprung at the tatterwing, deftly sliding beneath the sharp point as the dragon thrust the spear. He rose, his face inches from the dragon's toothy jaws, but before the creature could even think of biting him, he slipped his knife into the dragon's gut up to the hilt, then twisted. The dragon fell, dropping his spear. Bitterwood spun, catching the spear as it fell, throwing it with a fluid motion at the superstitious dragon who fled toward the door. The spear pierced the sky-dragon's spine and a childlike shriek tore from the creature's throat as he fell against the barn door, closing it.

The final dragon, the wounded one, stood stock still in the center of the barn, his golden eyes glinting in the gloom.

"Is this... is this... is this because of the widow?" he asked.

Bitterwood frowned.

"The widow? What did you do to the widow?"

"We... we know we didn't steal the goat like we promised," the dragon said.

"Promised?" said Bitterwood. "What promise?"

"D-did Priter send you?" the dragon asked, sounding hesitant.

"Priter? What does Priter have to do with this?"

"He's been paying us to steal from farms across the river," said the dragon. "I don't know why."

Bitterwood knew why. On their own, the dragons had been too scared of the guns to cross to the human side of the river, which couldn't have helped with Priter's business model of demanding bribes in exchange for protection.

"Has he paid earth-dragons, too? Did he send them after the hog you saw when you stole those chickens?"

"What hog?" the dragon asked. "Which chickens?"

"The night you were wounded. You saw a hog."

"The big one? Yes. I recall it."

"Did you tell any earth-dragon about it?"

"N-not that I can think of. Why would I?"

Bitterwood's heart sank. The dragon wasn't lying. There was something in his tone Bitterwood recognized. Something he'd heard before. Not fear. Resignation.

"You know I'm going to kill you," said Bitterwood.

"I know," said the dragon, wearily, lifting up his tattered wings. "And it will be mercy."

Bitterwood drew his bow and placed an arrow against the string. He was almost tempted to let the dragon live. The tatterwing couldn't fly, and now he couldn't walk without pain. His closest companions were dead, and a lone tatterwing stood little chance of surviving for long. The fact the dragon didn't fear death robbed the moment of any satisfaction.

He loosed the arrow all the same. He stood for several minutes, listening to the dragon's rasping breath as he bled out. That sound, the wet, gurgling sob, was a noise he was intimately familiar with. To the dark thing that lived inside him it was a kind of music.

But his quiet reverie was disturbed by the weight of his newfound knowledge. Humans and dragons, working together to enrich themselves. He'd seen such things before. Burke might have turned a blind eye toward his rangers lining their pockets with bribes, but he couldn't believe Burke knew the rangers had actually partnered with dragons. Priter and his crew were just three men. Certainly all the rangers weren't so corrupt.

But few or many, it mattered little. He'd come hunting the monsters who'd caused tears to well in Zeeky's eyes. The ghost of vengeance whispering in his ear demanded blood, and human blood and dragon blood would look the same when coating the shaft of one of his arrows. The job wasn't yet finished.

As he stood lost in thought, awareness slowly crept in. The roaring flames of the saloon, the chaotic shouts and screams in the distance, gave way to the nearby baying of ox-dogs drawing closer. They were right outside the barn, from the sound of it.

He stood still as a tombstone as something pushed against the barn door. The fallen body of the dragon he'd speared blocked the door, but the earth-dragon on the other side put his shoulder to the task and pushed the door open with a grunt.

The light of the burning tavern spilled through the door and lit Bitterwood, his brown cloak red in the firelight.

The earth-dragon looked at him dully. Behind the dragon were a pair of ox-dogs and at least twenty earth-dragons. They all grew quiet as they looked at him, his bow, and the dying tatterwing at his feet, still gurgling out his dying breaths.

The earth-dragon in the doorway broke the silence, saying, in despair, "You."

"I," said Bitterwood. "The shadow in the forest. The relentless river, and the rock, unmoving. I am the Death of All Dragons. It would be wise of you to run."

"We'll not run!" a large earth-dragon shouted from behind the ox-dogs. Then, there was a flash and a loud BANG, and the dragon in the doorway fell forward, the back of his head turned to pulp. Bitterwood didn't waste time contemplating exactly what had happened before he was in motion, diving toward the stalls, away from the light of the doorway as more explosions flashed and the wood of the barn wall splintered and tore. A tiny ball of hot lead tore through his boot cuff and lodged in his shin and he gasped.

Shotguns! Some of the dragons had Burke's weapons!

It made them bold as they charged through the door. But he was in shadows and they were in light. His bow sang sweetly and arrows whistled through the air and dragons fell. After the initial rush of five or six, the remaining dragons realized that entering the barn was suicide. Someone shouted, "Burn him out!"

Bitterwood put his fingers into his mouth and whistled. There was a clattering on the roof and the rafters creaked as the great weight of the long-wyrm launched into motion. Bitterwood jumped up, grabbing the edge of the hayloft, and ran toward the upper door overlooking the crowd.

He arrived in time to watch Skitter charge into the crowd, snarling and snapping, a tornado of claws and teeth. Bitterwood saw one of the earth-dragons armed with a shotgun take aim at the long-wyrm and put an arrow into the dragon's wrist before he could pull the trigger. The wounded dragon dropped his gun and it went off as it hit the ground, blasting a hole in the side of the nearest ox-dog.

For ten seconds, perhaps twelve, the earth-dragons stood their ground in the face of the strange beast tearing at their brothers, while the hail of arrows dropped fellow dragons left and right. Then they routed, and Bitterwood took out a few with arrows to the back, but decided against killing them all. He'd heard before the rumor that he'd been killed by Shandrazel and had been content to let the rumor spread. He'd thought it was time for the Ghost Who Kills to be laid to rest. Now, he wanted every dragon in the kingdom to know that Bitterwood had returned. For this purpose alone, a living dragon was more valuable than a dead one.

BITTERWOOD CAME TO DRAGON FORGE late at night, leaving Skitter a good distance away. The ground around the fort was barren and there was little cover for a beast of Skitter's size. Even an ordinary man would have been plainly visible on the open ground, but, Bitterwood knew how to move unseen. He scaled the walls effortlessly, even with the heavy burden he carried on his back.

Despite the late hour, there was revelry going on in the alleys where the liquor was sold. Burke insisted on operating the foundries all day and night, with the unintended consequence that he'd created a city where, since honest men had reason to be on the streets at night, less honorable men could move about freely as well. Bitterwood sniffed the air and frowned. Beneath the stench of the foundry was the unmistakable smell of pork fat dripping over hot coals.

He dropped down from the wall onto the cobblestone streets and walk without any effort to hide himself toward the establishment where the smell of the pork smoke was strongest. He walked past the door, his face concealed under his cloak, and glanced inside, confirming that several of Burke's rangers were there, drinking, smoking, and enjoying the company of women. He walked on, finding the nearest stable. As expected, he found a cart outside the door and an ox-dog sleeping beside it. He walked past the dog silently.

Inside the stable were thirty horses. He soon found the ones Priter, Bo, and Wessing had been riding. In a room attached to the stable he found saddles and saddle bags, and beside the saddle bags he found a pair of battle-axes. He went through the bags nearest the axes, wanting to be sure. After less than a minute of searching, he found what he was looking for. Muddy boots. Riveted to the soles of the boots were the wooden outlines of an earth-dragons print, crudely carved, but fixed with actual claws on the toes. In fine sand, he would have noticed they were fake at a glance, but in the trampled muck of a pig pen? He shook his head. That was no excuse. If he'd taken any time at all to study the prints, he would have noticed something was off. If he'd spent more time pondering how the dragons could have ridden along the road, or why they left behind the bodies of the dogs, the truth would have been plain. He hadn't wasted even a moment building a case against the dragons. He'd judged them guilty and declared himself executioner. He felt no remorse for the pile of corpses he'd left in Multon. The dragons had been guilty of life itself, an unpardonable sin.

Now that he knew which men had committed the crime, the proper thing to do would be to report the evidence to Burke. Especially given what he carried in the bundle strapped to his back, Burke would have no choice but to take action. But, would Burke hang a man for stealing a pig? Probably not. Would they be hanged for dealing with dragons? Perhaps. But it was the first crime that had made Zeeky cry. The dark ghost within Bitterwood had never demanded human blood before this night, and some small, feeble voice within him whispered it wasn't too late to turn back.

"It's been too late for a long time," the dark ghost answered.

Bitterwood walked from the stables back to the house where the rangers had been drinking. He'd counted nine men and seven women. All of the men had shotguns near them. If these had been dragons, he'd enter with his bow drawn and kill the lot of them before they could even register what was happening. But, while all the men and women were feasting on stolen meat, how many knew its origins?

He stepped into the door and stood there, motionless, staring across the crowd at Priter. One by one, the men and woman took notice of him, and one by one they stopped talking as they saw his face. The silence spread like a wave until the only one left talking was Priter, who said to the woman on his lap, "Let's take the bottle up to your room and..." Then he noticed the silence, noticed the turned heads of his brethren, and turned toward Bitterwood. For half a moment, his face went pale. Then, he rallied with a smile and rose, rudely pushing the woman from his lap. With his hand on his belt next to the sheath of his dagger, Priter said, with a forced friendliness, "Well, looky here. It's our friend the farmer come to join the party."

"No," said Bitterwood. "You are mistaken."

"Not here for the party?" said Priter, with a soft chuckle. "Too bad. We got some mighty fine barbeque."

"You're mistaken in believing I'm a farmer."

Priter's fingers closed around the hilt of his dagger. "You think I haven't heard the rumors? That you used to be some kind of badass dragon fighter? But how tough can you be if you came crying to Burke about losing a few chickens?"

Bitterwood said nothing.

"And, even if you were a fighter, once, you're old now, worn out. Join the party, farmer, or go home. What you choose matters nothing to me."

"Very well," said Bitterwood, drawing his bow and placing an arrow to the string.

All around him, men reached for their guns.

Bitterwood glanced around the room. "Consider your actions carefully. What you choose matters a great deal to me. I've come for Wessing, Bo, and Priter. There's no need for the rest of you to die as well. You may leave. Stay and defend these villains and I will show no mercy."

None of the rangers moved toward the door. All took aim with their shotguns, though some were so drunk that the barrels weren't quite pointed where he stood.

"You've all made your choice," said Bitterwood, taking aim at Priter. "You will not live to regret it."

"There are nine of us!" said Priter, sounding incredulous. "Put down your bow! Are you out of my mind?"

Bitterwood released his arrow. He'd aimed at Priter's right ear and neatly took off the top inch. Burke's shotguns had a delay of half a second once the trigger was pulled and the fuse ignited. He waited just long enough to assure everyone had braced for the kick of the gunpowder, then dove forward as thunder filled the room. Tiny stray balls of lead ripped through his cloak and a few peppered his ribs but did no real damage. However, he hadn't counted on the ringing in his ears deafening him. Ordinarily, when he fought multiple opponents, he could map their location in his mind by the sound of their panting even if he didn't have eyes on them.

He sprang up and delivered a vicious kick to Priter's face, using it as a springboard to spin in the air, to face the chaos of the greater room. One of the whores was dead on the floor, with little left of her face, a victim of a poorly aimed shot. The other women were rushing the door in a flurry of petticoats, with shrill shrieks he heard even above the ringing in his ears.

A few of the rangers to his right were reloading, an act that took several seconds, while it took him a fraction of a second to nock an arrow and release it. In the span of three seconds, four men were dead with arrows jutting from their hearts, including Bo.

To his left, three of the rangers, including Wessing were also wounded, victims of stray shot, but the fourth had tossed aside his gun and charged at Bitterwood with a short sword. Bitterwood dropped his bow, deftly dodging the blade then dropped the man with a punch to the throat, tearing his blade from his grasp, thrusting the tip into the man's back as he fell, targeting his right kidney.

Yanking the sword free he ran at the three wounded men. They threw up their hands to plead mercy, but

Bitterwood was beyond mercy. With three swift hacks, the men fell to his feet, bleeding profusely from wounds to their necks.

Bitterwood spun back around to Priter, who'd seen none of this, since he was clutching his broken nose with both hands, his eyes clenched shut with pain.

Bitterwood grabbed Priter by his collar.

"No," said Bitterwood, his voice sounding hollow and distant through the ringing in his ears. "No, I am not out of my mind. Killing you is the most rational thing I'll do this night. Let a thief get away without consequences and all other thieves will only grow bolder."

Priter forced his eyes open. By now, he had to have noticed the unnatural silence of the room. His eyes went wide as he saw the dead bodies of his companions, alive not even twenty seconds ago.

"I'll confess it all!" Priter cried. "I'll tell Burke all I've done!"

"You think I came to let another man kill you?" Bitterwood said through clenched teeth. "You'll not die swiftly, Priter."

"He'll not die at all," said a woman's voice behind him.

Bitterwood froze. He knew the voice.

"Put him down," said Anza.

"You got here fast," Bitterwood grumbled.

"So many guns going off at once wakes one swiftly," said Anza. "And from my bedroom window, this place is only three rooftops away."

Bitterwood grimaced. He didn't want to fight Anza. First, as a rule, he didn't like fighting women, and second, if there was anyone in Dragon Forge who might actually harm him, it was Anza.

Bitterwood turned his head and found Anza in the doorway wearing only a cotton slip. In one hand she carried a tomahawk, in the other a longsword. The muscles in her arms and shoulders were tight, ready for action. It would not be easy to get past her if he was dragging Priter.

Anza kept her eyes fixed on him, but he could see in her face that she was making an account of all the dead bodies.

"What have you done?" she asked, her voice filled with confusion.

"I've rid your father of thieves and traitors living under his nose," said Bitterwood.

Anza's back straightened and her eyes grew hard. "I can't let you walk away from this."

"Tell her what you took from me," Bitterwood said to Priter.

"He's crazy!" Priter screamed. "He just came in and started killing people! I never did anything to him!"

Bitterwood used his short sword to cut off the tip of Priter's other ear, then spun, his hand outstretched, and caught the tomahawk Anza hurled before it could bury itself in his skull.

"I don't want to fight you," said Bitterwood, as Anza grasped her longsword with both hands.

"I enjoy a challenge," Anza said, coolly, though she didn't follow her words with an attack. She'd witnessed his reflexes, and had to know any attack she made would be parried. She would wait for Bitterwood to make the first move, since he would be at his most vulnerable when he was thrusting his own blade or retrieving his bow. Bitterwood pushed Priter in front of him and held a sword to his throat. "Tell her!"

"It was just a pig!" Priter screamed. "It was just a damned pig!"

"Poocher?" said Anza, her face growing slack.

Bitterwood nodded.

Anza's face hardened again. "I liked Poocher. He helped me defeat Vulpine. But I can't turn a blind eye to these bodies. You'll go to the gallows for what you've done."

"Perhaps you value the lives of pig thieves," said Bitterwood. "But your rangers have betrayed you, trading with the dragons at Multon."

"What are you talking about?"

Bitterwood lowered his sword, moving cautiously as he reached for the bundle on his back. He'd wrapped the items in a burlap sack in the barn in Multon, and now held the edge of the sack as he tossed it forward, unfurling it. A pair of shotguns clattered to the floor.

"Dragons used these against me in Multon. I'm sure there are more to be found. Someone among the rangers has been trading guns for whiskey or women or something else. I didn't have much of an opportunity to ask questions. But if the earth-dragons have guns, it won't be long before the College of Spires figures out how to make their own weapons."

Anza frowned as she stared at the guns.

"What do you know of this?" she asked, her eyes fixed on Priter.

"Nothing!" Priter cried. "I swear, I wasn't trading guns! There are lots of humans going to Multon! It could have been anyone!"

"Truly?" Bitterwood said, placing his blade across the man's throat. "You have nothing of further value to tell us?"

"I swear I had nothing to do with trading guns!"

Bitterwood slit the man's throat and pushed him away.

He stared at Anza. "If Burke wishes to hang me, it may as well be for nine dead men instead of eight. Now stand aside, girl."

"I'm not afraid of you," she said, tightening her grip on her blade, moving lightly on her feet as she stepped back from the pool of blood spreading from Priter's body.

"Perhaps you aren't afraid," he said. "But I am."

"Afraid of me?" she asked.

"Of myself," he said. "This morning, as I rode into market, I'd convinced myself I would never kill a dragon again, let alone a fellow man. But murder and death are all I've known for twenty years. A few months as a farmer cannot change who I truly am. I will kill you, Anza, if you try to stop me from leaving."

"No you won't," she said, charging him as he'd anticipated.

She moved like water, swift and fluid, faster than anyone he'd fought in a long time. Burke had trained Anza since she could walk in the art of combat, and her mastery with a sword was unrivaled. But she'd lost her cool, goaded by his threat, her mind no doubt in turmoil because of the revelation that the dragons were getting guns, and no matter how well trained she was in combat, she had to feel at least a flicker of fear due to knowledge that Bitterwood had killed nine armed men with such ease.

The hesitation of even a hundredth of a second as she swung her sword was more than enough for Bitterwood to parry her blade with his own, knock aside the hidden dagger she'd produced using the tomahawk he still held, then deliver a fierce head-butt that left bright sparks dancing before his eyes but left her sprawled on the ground, bleeding from her nose.

As she rolled over, groaning, he retrieved his bow.

"I could have killed you," he said, as she struggled to find her feet. "But I need you to tell Burke about the guns, and also that his rangers are stealing from the farmers they've sworn to protect. Tell him to fix these things, or I'll fix them for him."

Then he calmly walked through the door and into the alley. A crowd had gathered, including dozens of armed men. He glared at them and said nothing as he walked. One by one, they stepped from his path.

"Bitterwood," he heard someone whisper. "That's Bitterwood!"

"Bitterwood," another answered.

"Bitterwood!" a dozen voices said at once.

All in the same tone of fear that had always given him such pleasure when voice by dragons. Among mankind, his name had been whispered in hope, or shouted in defiance into the faces of dragons. No more.

All the blood and death and terrible secrets uncovered that night would never haunt him as much as those voices of fear.

BITTERWOOD'S WHOLE BODY ached by the time he reached the cabin. Priter had been right about one thing. He was old. In the heat of the moment, fueled by hate, pain was a distant, trivial thing. Now, every tiny ball of lead in his muscles burned with each jostle as Skitter scurried across uneven ground. His arms felt weighted down by heavy shackles. His body, finely tuned and full of life when killing, became an unspeakable burden in the remorse that followed.

But an even greater burden than his body was his heart. What had he done this evening? In blindly pursuing revenge, he'd thrown everything away. Burke wasn't going to ignore the slaughter of nine rangers. If Burke sent a hundred men after him, what then? Even if he could kill them all, should he? As much as he hated his fellow men this night, he still hated dragons more, and fighting Burke was the same as fighting on the side of the dragons.

He rode Skitter into the barn. Lights flickered in the windows of the cabin. The children were still awake, or at least they'd left the lanterns burning.

He should go without saying a word.

No. He should say good-bye first.

Which was the kinder option? To vanish without explanation, leaving his fate unknown, or to say good-bye, and try to justify why he had to abandon them?

Were he not so tired, he might have had the strength to ride on without looking back, to live off the land once more, alone. But, in his weariness, he could think of a dozen small things within the cabin that would make is life alone once more moderately more bearable. And, at least the children would know what he had done, and that they weren't at fault for his leaving. Plus, if he was to abandon them, he should at least try to see to their futures. Burke had no reason to hate the children. He would write a letter, telling Burke to sell his farm and use the money to see that the children were taken care of. Burke was an honorable man and would do the right thing for innocent children, if asked.

Bitterwood walked across the barnyard to the cabin. He stood for a long time at the door. He was almost ready to turn around when Zeeky said, softly, "You might as well come in."

He opened the door. He half expected that Jeremiah would be asleep, since the boy could sleep through almost anything, but he was awake, sitting at the table with Zeeky, the cabin's lone lantern lit above them, painting their faces in pale shades. They both looked tired and scared. It was plain both had been crying.

"Dragons didn't kill Poocher," Bitterwood said, though he couldn't explain why he had to say it.

"I know," Zeeky said, swallowing hard. "If I'd... I was so angry but... dragons wouldn't have left the dogs. And, after you left, I went out to the pen, and the footprints... they were all wrong. They weren't deep enough."

Bitterwood nodded.

"Which means you killed a lot of dragons for no reason at all," she said, sounding on the verge of tears. "And it's all my fault!"

Bitterwood hadn't even considered this might upset her. But she was so tenderhearted she wouldn't even eat the fish he and Jeremiah caught. Until she'd handed him his bow, she'd never wanted to hurt any other living thing. The thought that she had caused the death of even dragons had to be tearing her apart.

"I had reason," he said. "The only reason I've ever needed. They were dragons."

"And what?" said Zeeky. "Every dragon in the world deserves to die? You were friends with Hex. Jandra was raised by a dragon. Would you kill them?"

"You don't understand," he said.

"I think I do," she said. "And so be it. If you have to kill dragons, so be it. Just promise me you'll always come home to us."

Bitterwood's mouth went dry. He couldn't even move his jaw. Zeeky, watching his face, grew pale.

"You were gone a long time," said Jeremiah, before Zeeky could say anything.

Bitterwood nodded.

"Did you find the men who took Poocher?" he asked.

Bitterwood nodded again.

Jeremiah asked, "Did you—"

"Yes," said Bitterwood. "I killed them."

"Oh no," said Zeeky, instantly grasping the ramifications.

Jeremiah, though, didn't seem to see past his immediate satisfaction with Bitterwood's answer. "Good."

"No," said Bitterwood. "Burke won't let what I did pass easily. I'm sorry, but I—"

"You can't go," said Zeeky, rising with clenched fists.

"If I stay, they'll hang me," said Bitterwood.

"They can't even come onto the farm," said Zeeky, half sobbing, half snarling. "I'll tell Skitter to kill anyone who tries to lay a hand on you!"

Bitterwood's eyes went wide as he saw the violent passions that filled her once gentle frame.

"They can't punish you!" said Jeremiah. "They killed Poocher! You didn't hurt anyone who didn't have it coming!"

Bitterwood shook his head. "I'm sorry. Burke will know the two of you aren't guilty of anything. His men won't hurt you. I'll going to write him a letter telling him to sell the land and put the money aside for you. He'll find you a new home."

"We're coming with you," said Zeeky. "Skitter can carry the three of us, easy."

"No," said Bitterwood. "I've lived as a fugitive. It's not an easy life."

"Can't be harder than farming," grumbled Jeremiah.

"I've survived as a runaway before," said Zeeky. "I can do it again."

Bitterwood pulled the third chair out from the table and sat wearily.

"Are you hurt?" asked Jeremiah.

"They shot you?" said Zeeky, looking at his blood soaked clothes.

"I've live through worse," said Bitterwood. "But nothing worse than telling the two of you goodbye. We've not lived together long, but I want you to know you're my son and daughter. If I could step back to this morning and change my actions, I would. But, Zeeky, you saw it. There's something inside me. Something that loves killing. If it hadn't been tonight, it would have come out another night. I was not put on this world to be happy. Leaving you is the only way forward."

"It's not forward," said Zeeky. "It's backward. You're going back to who you used to be!"

"Where else am I to go?" he asked.

"Back to Dragon Forge," said Zeeky. "Talk to Burke. Tell him why you did what you did."

"It's not that simple," said Bitterwood.

"It would be if you rode back on Skitter with me," said Zeeky. "They wouldn't shoot at me, would they?"

"They might," said Bitterwood.

"If they tried to hurt you or Zeeky or even Skitter, I'd kill them," said Jeremiah.

"What?" said Bitterwood.

"I'd kill anyone who tried to hurt our family," Jeremiah repeated.

Bitterwood almost laughed. Jeremiah was so quiet, and had, to his knowledge, run from every fight he'd ever been around. But... was he so different at Jeremiah's age? He'd been small and slight, bullied by his older brother, no one's picture of a fighter. But something changed within him after the dragons came and killed his whole village. If he'd been a great brawler like his brother, perhaps he would have died early on. He might have entered into fights with confidence and bravery. Bitterwood, on the other hand, had no skills in combat back then, so he'd fought the war with methods others would describe as cowardly, killing unsuspecting dragons with a bow from a distance, then running. The warrior who'd fought so many this evening hadn't been born overnight. It had taken years of close calls and a lot of luck to learn to survive hand to hand combat with multiple enemies.

"Jeremiah," he said, calmly, "Burke and his rangers aren't to blame for the men I killed. Their blood is on my hands."

"They're corrupt," said Jeremiah.

"Some are," said Bitterwood. "But, what if among a hundred rangers there are five honest men? What if there's only one? Would you want to be the man who killed him?"

"What if you killed him tonight?" asked Zeeky.

"The men I killed tonight weren't honorable," said Bitterwood. "But that doesn't mean I was right to kill them."

The full weight of what he said weighed heavy on him. He shook his head. "I was wrong."

"But Poocher—" said Zeeky.

"Was a pig," said Bitterwood. "You must see the difference between a man and a pig."

"Yeah," said Zeeky. "Pigs don't slaughter men and eat them."

Bitterwood allowed himself half a grin at her logic, then said, "No point in putting it off. Bring me the pen and book you use for your studies so I can write the letter. I have to be gone before sunrise."

"You don't have until sunrise," said Zeeky. "They're coming now."

"What?" said Bitterwood.

She nodded. "Can't you feel the horses galloping?" She had her bare feet firmly on the packed earth of the floor. "A lot of them. Too many to count. We've got to run!"

"Get to the barn!" Bitterwood shouted. "Get on Skitter!"

Like that, it was decided. He couldn't leave them behind. He couldn't take them back to his old life, living on the run, hunting dragons. But with Skitter, they could be far away in days. Maybe back down south, to the land where he'd been born, where people probably hadn't even heard of the rebellion. They could start a new life, start a new farm...

You cannot run forever, the voice inside him said sternly.

Zeeky paused a moment, grabbing a sack and shoving her books inside, but Bitterwood tore the sack away and tossed it to the floor. "There's no time to take anything. Go!"

They ran outside. The hooves of the horses could be heard now. It sounded as if every ranger left in the town had turned out to capture him. If capture was their intention. Worse, the horses weren't just on the road. They were trampling through the corn and were crashing through the woods, converging on the farm from all directions except the river.

"Hurry!" he cried, leading the children toward the barn.

Then, BANG! BANG! BANG! Shots rang out from the direction of the cornfield. Jeremiah gasped in pain and fell. Zeeky slid to a stop and ran back for him. Bitterwood wheeled about and beat her to the fallen boy, who'd been shot in the knee. Jeremiah cried out in pain as Bitterwood lifted him. There was no way to carry him without bending his knee.

More shots rang out, the lead balls whistling all around them. Men on horseback had little hope of a steady aim, but Bitterwood knew one moment of bad luck might bring an end to any of them. "Get inside the barn!" he yelled to Zeeky. The girl obeyed, throwing open the barn door and bolting inside. Then, Zeeky yelped in shock and surprise.

Bitterwood ran into the barn and found Zeeky floating in mid-air upside down. There was a rope around her ankle. She'd stepped into a snare. Someone had reached the barn first and set a trap.

"Go on without me!" Zeeky cried.

Bitterwood stopped. There was only one person quiet enough and fast enough to have reached the barn before the rest of Burke's men. If she was in the barn, the rangers wouldn't be shooting into it. But, once he was on Skitter, and outside the barn, the air would be full of shot from all directions.

"The boy's hurt," Bitterwood said. "Promise me he'll be cared for."

"The children have done nothing wrong," said Anza, in the darkness. His eyes followed upward to find her shadowy form in the rafters. She carried one of the skywall bows. It was drawn, with an arrow aimed at his head. She was skilled enough not to hit the boy.

"Anza!" Zeeky yelled. "Put down your bow or I'll sic Skitter on you. He'll tear you to ribbons!"

"Even that beast isn't fast enough to stop me from releasing this arrow," said Anza.

Bitterwood's heart sank. Not because of Anza's threat, but because he believed Zeeky really would kill to protect him. What had he done? How could he have been so blind to consequences?

"Why haven't you killed me already?" he asked, his eyes still locked on Anza.

"My father insists on laws," said Anza. "You will be fairly tried."

"What's the point of a trial?" he asked. "You know I'm guilty."

"The rangers outside need little prodding to become a mob," said Anza. "If I throw you to them now, they'll lynch you. My father would be better served if you faced a lawful execution following a trial. You'll be a useful lesson for those who wish to take the law into their own hands."

"Don't listen to her!" said Zeeky. "You can still get away!"

Bitterwood knelt and placed Jeremiah on the ground. The boy was sobbing in his pain, too distraught for words.

Bitterwood put up his hands and said, "I'm your prisoner."

"Why?" Zeeky cried. "Why?"

"It's futile to run," he said. "They'll kill me, and what lesson would you and Jeremiah take away?" He shook his head. "Anza's right. I've broken the law. I must pay a price. Your future is with the men and women of the rebellion. I'm doing this to save you from the deadly things I've fought with all these years."

"The dragons," said Anza, dropping down from the rafters.

"Myself," said Bitterwood, offering her his hands, "and my ghosts."

HURT

HURT

HER FATHER'S EYES revealed his thoughts more clearly than his words, Anza thought.

To a casual listener, Burke sounded calm, even disinterested, as he spoke to the shackled and bruised prisoner on his knees before him.

"You're going to be hung, Cain," Burke said, in the same tones he might have used to say, "It's going to rain later," or "I think it's time for lunch." But in Burke's eyes, Anza saw hatred, contempt, and something close to rage. Beneath this, in the way he stood and breathed, in the stiffness of his neck and the tension of his torso, she saw something more terrible. Her father was afraid, and not with a fear that pushes a man to fight. Instead, her father stared into a pit of bottomless despair he might never climb out from if he toppled.

"I didn't do anything!" Cain screamed, the iron chain around his neck rattling. "I tell you I lost the gun!"

"No," said Burke. "Two weeks ago you reported that your gun had misfired and that the barrel had split apart. You said you tossed it into the river so that the three earth-dragons pursuing you couldn't get their hands on it, then proceeded to fight them off with your sword. It was quite the tale of heroism. You even had the scabs and bruises to show from the fight."

"Because it really happened!" said Cain.

Burke nodded. "I believe a fight happened. But you weren't fighting dragons. You got into a fight with the man you were riding with, Jubal. You told us the dragons killed him, and you didn't know what had happened to his rifle."

"I swear that's the truth!"

"Burke," said the third man in the room, standing next to the door, looking doubtful. "I've known Cain a long time. He's a god-fearing man, one of Ragnar's first converts. Why would you— "

Burke glowered at the speaker, his stern expression bringing the big man to silence. The new focus of her father's disapproval was Stonewall, captain of the rangers, and the man who'd assured Burke that Cain could be trusted when the gun had first gone missing. Stonewall wasn't an easy man to intimidate. He was unnaturally tall, seven feet if not a few inches more, with a muscular build that made him look as solid as his namesake.

"Stonewall, you said you'd checked out his story," said Burke.

"I had no reason to doubt his word. I still don't."

"Your blind trust in this fool might doom us all."

Stonewall didn't respond to this, but his face was easy to read. He still hoped that Cain was innocent, that everything was a misunderstanding. At the same time, in the fine lines around his eyes and mouth, she saw a second emotion. *Guilt.* Part of him worried that the accusations were true, and the failure to discover Cain's treachery before now was entirely his fault. Anza felt sorry for Stonewall. She'd fought side by side with him when breaking Vulpine's siege of Dragon Forge. He'd saved her life. She had no question of his courage and integrity, and still thought her father had chosen well in appointing him commander of the rangers. Stonewall was a good man, but this goodness was perhaps his greatest flaw. He assumed an innate decency in all men. This was in stark contrast to her father, who viewed his fellow men as engineering problems, riddled with unseen flaws that would inevitably cause them to fail.

Burke trusted no one fully save for Anza. He'd trained her in both body and mind to be a living machine, an instrument he could rely on to do whatever he needed done. From an early age, she'd understood the unusual nature of their relationship. After all, he'd explained it carefully and deliberately. The role she was to play in his life had been spelled out with flawless logic.

Now, Burke would educate Stonewall with the same blunt approach. Burke nodded toward Anza. She handed him the two rifles she carried. Burke stepped toward Stonewall. "These were recovered from the village of Multon. The dragons there have enslaved human women to serve as whores, and distill whiskey from grains given to them so they could make bread. Where there are whores and whiskey, there are men willing to pay any price for one or both."

"I know this," said Stonewall. "I'm doing all I can to stop it."

"You're not doing enough," said Burke.

"I don't even drink!" said Cain. Anza thought it was foolish for him to speak while her father had turned his attention to Stonewall. Stonewall had disappointed Burke, but Cain had betrayed the rebellion, and anything he said only brought him one step closer to the noose.

Burke handed one of the guns to Stonewall and continued holding the other.

"Bitterwood brought these back from Multon."

Stonewall frowned as he studied the gun.

"I... I haven't even been to Multon!" said Cain.

"I've found men who say you have," Burke said, turning back to the prisoner. "I've also found witnesses who say you and Jubal got into a fight over a whore and that you shot him in cold blood. The men who witnessed this couldn't speak since doing so would mean admitting that they were doing business with dragons. One of these dragons probably convinced you that they could earn a few coins by making sure the truth of what happened reached me. In exchange for silence, you surrendered the guns."

"Lies," said Cain. "Who speaks such slander? Stonewall, you know me! I would never do such a thing!"

"Then how do you explain that I'm holding your shotgun?" asked Burke, holding up the weapon. "The gun you swore you'd thrown into the river after the barrel split apart?"

"That's not my gun!" said Cain. "Your guns all look the same. It could belong to anyone!"

Before coming into the room, Burke had removed the screws that secured the wooden stock. He slipped off the stock and turned the gun so that a series of numbers were revealed on the metal beneath. "It's not widely known, but each shotgun is stamped with an identifying mark that's hidden by the stock. To date, we've manufactured four hundred and forty-two guns based on my original design. Thirty-nine of these weapons have been ruined, usually because the barrel fails. Three hundred ninety-eight guns are accounted for in the hands of rangers and guardsmen. Five are lost, and I've foolishly trusted Stonewall to investigate what happened. Ultimately though, I'm responsible. I wanted to believe that fellow men wouldn't betray the rebellion by selling our most priceless advantage to our mortal enemies. I clung to hope despite my long years of experience."

Cain licked his lips. His eyes darted around the room, from the gun, to Anza, to Stonewall, then the floor. "I... I must have been mistaken," he said, his throat sounding dry. "The dragons were attacking from all sides. When the gun misfired, there was so much smoke... maybe the barrel didn't split. I swear, I threw it into the river! The dragons must have fished it out!"

Burke turned away. "You'll be able to tell your story at trial. Now that we've confronted the witnesses who were there that night, we've got four men who'll testify to what actually happened. My daughter can be very persuasive."

"You mean she's tortured people into saying what you want them to say!" said Cain.

"Have you tortured witnesses, Anza?" asked Stonewall, sounding troubled.

"No," she said, instantly wondering why she said it. It was technically true, yes. Holding a knife to a man's throat was intimidation, not torture. Still, only the fact that everyone she'd questioned had succumbed to threats had kept her from hurting anyone. Cain's bruises were the only bodily harm she'd inflicted, and that only because he'd tried to run.

"You lying bitch!" snapped Cain. "Everyone knows the truth about you! Everyone hates you! You're a damned monster!"

Burke slipped the wooden butt back onto the gun, took a step forward, and smashed Cain's mouth with the improvised club. Cain fell to his side, spitting blood.

"For betraying mankind, I intend to hang you," said Burke. "Insult my daughter again and you'll never make it to a noose. I'll cut your damned tongue from your mouth and let you choke on your own blood."

Cain didn't answer, though Anza could see he was still aware of every word. Stonewall looked deeply unhappy, but she couldn't tell if it was because of her father's violence toward a helpless man or because he was now accepting the reality that he'd been wrong.

Burke glanced at Anza and said, calmly, "Put this traitor in the cell with Bitterwood."

Anza nodded, understanding at once that anger had won out over fear within her father. He'd stepped back from the pit of despair and was now thinking through the problem before him.

Stonewall said, "Bitterwood will murder him."

"What of it?" said Burke.

"Cain deserves a trial, and, given the evidence against him, an execution. Handing him over to Bitterwood is no different than handing him over to a lynch mob."

Burke turned his back to Stonewall. He let out a long, slow breath. "Fine. He'll have his own cell."

"I've heard Bitterwood brought back three guns," said Stonewall. "I'll organize the rangers at once to raid Multon and find the other two."

Burke shook his head. "An army riding into Multon is only going to alert the dragons that we're on to them. They'll have all the time they need to either run or conceal the guns where we can't find them. Anza will go alone, tonight, to fix this."

"No," said Stonewall. "I'll go. I'm responsible. No one should be put in danger because of my mistakes."

Burke said, "Anza is more than capable of—"

"We'll both go," said Anza. Her father looked shocked. She was slightly shocked as well. She worked best in silence and shadows. Stonewall was a competent fighter, but no one would describe him as inconspicuous. Having him accompany her was a risk, but it was a risk she was willing to take, for reasons that would be difficult to explain if her father asked questions.

"Very well," said Burke. He turned to Stonewall. "I suppose you deserve a chance to redeem yourself. Help Anza bring back those guns. Kill any dragon you find who's even laid eyes on the weapons. And since you're the only one in this room who believes in God, it can't hurt for you to pray that we're not too late."

NIGHT HAD FALLEN when Anza and Stonewall flew over the village of Multon. There was only a thin sliver of moon, but in the cloudless night it was enough to cast their shadows on the rooftops, two human silhouettes with wings like eagles. A superstitious observer looking up at that moment could have been forgiven for believing he'd seen angels.

There was nothing supernatural about the wings Anza and Stonewall wore. According to her father, they were artifacts of now lost technology. Anza didn't truly understand how the silver wings worked. She suspected her father didn't either. They were attached to a large silver disk that adhered to Anza's back without straps, and required little conscious thought to use. You just set your eyes on a point where you wished to go and the wings would carry you there in utter silence. Unlike dragon wings, her wings didn't flap, though they bent and folded to catch the air to steer her.

She led Stonewall toward a burned out shell of a building, landing in the shadows behind it. With a thought, the silver wings folded compactly back into the disks they wore, safely out of the way, making soft, musical chiming noises as they did so. Ordinarily, she liked the wind chime sound of the wings opening and closing, but on a stealth mission the noise sounded dangerously loud. She looked around the corner of the building, studying to make sure no one had heard them. Seeing no one, she glanced at Stonewall, indicating with her eyes that he should follow. They darted along the back of a neighboring building. She moved lightly, nearly soundless in her moccasins. Stonewall did his best to be quiet, but his giant boots thumped as he followed, and she questioned the wisdom of bringing him along, though didn't yet regret it.

The simple truth was, she liked Stonewall. She had no other friends at Dragon Forge. Women shunned her and men feared her. Stonewall always treated her decently. They saw each other frequently in the course of their duties and he always took time to talk to her, even though she possessed no capacity at all to engage in what was sometimes called "small talk." She'd grown up mute, unable to speak due to a tumor in her throat, until the tumor had been removed a few months ago. She'd gained control of her newfound voice with the same discipline she brought to the control of the rest of her body, but found most of the babble of conversations she overheard to be utterly pointless. Why anyone bothered to discuss the weather befuddled her. What was the use of stating that it was hot, or that it was raining, or that it was windy? Both speaker and listener were observing the same weather.

Yet, somehow, it was different with Stonewall. For him to say it was a sunny day made the day feel sunnier. He also told her about his life as the son of a fisherman in a village on the Drifting Isles. The hard work had left him strong, but he would sheepishly confess to her that he didn't think himself to be much of a fighter. He honestly hadn't had much practice. With his size, no one dared to attack him and he was too soft spoken and good natured to pick any fights himself. She'd offered to train him, but he'd been worried he'd hurt her, and though she'd rolled her eyes at the thought, she'd let the matter rest. What Stonewall lacked in combat finesse, he made up for with sheer muscle. With his mace, Stonewall could bash through the defenses of even the most heavily armored earth-dragons.

And on an underlying level she was still attempting to puzzle out, those same muscles made him... pleasant to look at. Even more than his impressive physicality, she liked his face, the openness of it, the way he freely smiled, even the way he'd shown his grief and guilt when confronted with Cain's duplicity, so different from the taciturn coolness of her father, or, for that matter, herself. Burke had trained Anza to use her emotions like tools. Fear was fuel to fight, happiness was her reward when she'd served her father well. Her feelings had been shaped with the same clockwork functionality as her muscles, so it brought both consternation and excitement that Stonewall stirred emotions she'd never experienced. All she knew of romance she'd learned from books; they proved a poor guide for defining what she felt. Stonewall didn't set her heart aflutter, nor did thoughts of him consume her every waking moment. But she did find pleasure in his company, even now, when attempting to move unnoticed with him at her heels was roughly the same challenge as remaining unseen while being followed by an ox.

They reached the rear of a two story building. The windows were open to let in the summer night breeze and the large room on the main floor danced with shadow and light from a dozen lanterns. The voices of dragons and humans, both men and women, could be heard. A woman was laughing in a false, wearied tone that indicated she had a financial incentive to find a cloddish male companion witty. The smell of strong whiskey wrinkled Anza's nose.

She motioned for Stonewall to stay hidden at the back of the building. She crept beneath the nearest window, staying low, and whistled the trilling song of a whip-poor-will, a night bird common to the area. She repeated the call three times, then crept back to the rear of the house.

"Are you sure he's inside?" whispered Stonewall.

"No," said Anza. "And if he is, who knows if he's awake? He's trustworthy, but at his age he does tend to nod off even when surrounded by noisy crowds."

"Ish 'cause of my age that no one thinks twice about speaking freely around me," said a familiar voice as the door at the back of the house swung open. "Also, most folks my age are half-deaf. I still hear as good as I did when I was your age, Anza."

An old man stepped onto the stairs with an unsteady foot. He swayed as he came down to the ground, reeking of whiskey and tobacco. He spread his arms and, in a slurred voice said, "Ish good to see you, Anza." He wrapped his arms around her in a hug that seemed as much to keep him from toppling over as to greet her.

"It's good to see you too, Thorny," she said, returning the embrace. Thorny was her father's oldest friend, and during her childhood he'd been the one person willing to hug her freely. Thorny was the closest thing she had to family other than her father.

"When Burke told me he had a spy inside Multon, I didn't expect it to be you," Stonewall said, looking concerned.

"You think I'm too old for such work?" asked Thorny, pulling back from Anza but keeping a hand on her shoulder to steady himself.

"I think you're too much of a drunkard," said Stonewall. "I've not seen you fully sober since the day we defeated Vulpine."

"Whish is why I'm the right man for the job," said Thorny, with a crooked grin that revealed his yellowed teeth, at least the few he had left. "Set me in a rocking chair in a tavern and no one takes a second look at me, even though they know I'm Burke's friend. The dragons aren't scared of me, because I'm old, and because of these." He held up his hands, twisted and gnarled by arthritis. "A drunken old cripple might as well be invisible around here. People feel free to say anything around me because it looks like I'm passed out drunk about half the time, even though I'm not."

"You're not really drunk?" asked Stonewall.

"I'm not really passed out," said Thorny. "I can drink an earth-dragon under the table. Nobody holds hish liquor better than me."

"We all have our talents," said Anza. "Father said to tell you we've no more time. Bitterwood took three rifles off the earth-dragons last night. He said he thinks there are more. Do you know who has them?"

"Sure do," said Thorny. "I wished I could have gotten word back to Burke, but Lark never showed up this morning for me to pass on what I've learned."

"Lark's dead," said Anza.

"The dragons got him?"

"Lark tried to defend a fellow ranger against Bitterwood," said Stonewall.

"Bitterwood!" said Thorny. He winced when he realized how loud he'd been, looking back at the door. "Bitterwood," he said again, in a whisper. "He was here last night! Burned down the big saloon. Killed twenty dragons like it was nothing, then rode off on that big weird snake of his."

"We know," said Anza. "What we didn't know was that there were guns here. Why didn't you tell us?"

"Because I didn't know until they pulled them out when they went after Bitterwood. Not that the guns did 'em any good. The bullets just went right through him like he was made of smoke. I've always heard he was a ghost. I guess it's true."

"He's no ghost," said Stonewall. "He's just a man, with a neck that will fit into a noose for what he's done."

Thorny looked skeptical. "Why would—"

"It's not important," said Anza, looking around to make sure they were still unseen. "All that matters now is that we get our hands on any guns the dragons still possess. Tell me you know something."

"Sure, I know something," said Thorny, grinning. "Look, for a few weeks, valkyries have been going in and out of Bigmouth's place almost every day. Word is, he's got something valuable he's trying to sell them, but they won't agree to his price."

"Bigmouth?" asked Stonewall.

"He's the earth-dragon who runs this town, more or less. I think his real name is Bimgrath or something like that, but everyone just calls him Bigmouth. He's a lot smarter than most earth-dragons. Used to be one of the dragon king's Black Silence assassins. He was born with the camouflage mutation that lets him blend in like a chameleon. Now that he's been running Multon for a few months, raking in money from whiskey and his stable of whores, it's kind of gone to his head. Doesn't see why he needs a winged dragon giving him orders. A year ago, any earth-dragon would have obeyed a sky-dragon without asking a question. Bigmouth knows he's got something valuable with those guns, and wants to make sure he gets something more valuable in return."

"What's he want?" asked Stonewall.

"Dragon Forge," said Thorny. "He knows that the endgame once the sky-dragons figure out how to make guns is the defeat of the human rebellion and the capture of Dragon Forge. He wants to be appointed leader of the town. But, get this, rumor is, he doesn't want to be in charge of the forge to follow orders from other dragons. He wants to run the forge so he'll control all the weaponry in the kingdom, command his own army, and declare himself king."

"This sounds like a political career we should nip in the bud," said Stonewall. "Where would we find this Bigmouth?"

"He's holed up in the rock house on the hill," said Thorny, motioning across the rolling hills with his gnarled hands. In the faint moonlight, a single house stood on a hilltop above the town. Even from this distance, Anza could see a dozen large earth-dragons around the house, standing guard.

"He seems cautious," said Stonewall.

"I told you he's smart," said Thorny. "And since he used to be an assassin, he's also paranoid. He thinks the valkyries might give up on negotiations and straight up attack him."

"These are also rumors you've heard?" asked Stonewall.

"Naw," said Thorny. "Bigmouth told me himself! He knows who I am. He's heard I'm on friendly terms with Burke. He's personally paid for my whiskey and had long talks finding out anything I know about wha's going on inside Dragon Forge."

"What do you tell him?" asked Stonewall.

"Stuff that keeps him nervous," said Thorny with a grin. "He thinks we've got a lot more armed men inside than we really do."

"If he trusts you enough to talk to you, do you think you can get the location of the guns out of him?" asked Stonewall.

128 - James Maxey

"Naw," said Thorny. "Since Bitterwood burned the big saloon, Bigmouth hasn't left his house. Word is Bitterwood's attack spooked him. I don't know if it's true or not, but I'm told he might settle for less the next time the valkyries show up, just to get rid of the guns."

Anza asked, "Last night, when Bitterwood attacked... where did the armed dragons come from?"

"The big saloon. In all the commotion, I lost track of where the guns went afterward."

"Wouldn't they be up in the rock house with him?" asked Stonewall.

"Maybe," said Thorny. "But maybe not. It's sort of the obvious place to look, and Bigmouth's no dummy."

"But Bigmouth knows where the guns are," said Anza.

"I can't imagine he doesn't," said Thorny.

"Then we should send you up to see him," said Stonewall. "If the valkyries won't barter for the guns, maybe we can."

Anza gave him a withering glance. "You're joking."

Stonewall crossed his arms over his chest. "I'm not joking. Bigmouth has ambitions that winged dragons will do their best to quash. If he doesn't think the valkyries are going to go along with his plan, we can give him something he wants."

"We aren't giving him Dragon Forge," said Anza.

"Of course not. But what do we have to lose by seeing if he'll haggle? If we just barge in and kill him, we might never find the guns."

"I won't kill him until it's time to kill him," said Anza. "You didn't look happy earlier when we talked about torture. But just because I didn't need to torture Cain doesn't mean I lack talent for the work. Bigmouth will tell us where the guns are when I'm done with him."

"You can see how well guarded his house is from here," said Stonewall. "There's no way we'll take out that many guards silently. He'll know we're coming."

"All the better," said Anza, unfolding her wings. She rose a foot into the air, locked eyes with Stonewall, and said, in a stern tone, "He'll be even more eager to talk once he sees what I've done to his protectors." Then she turned her eyes toward the stars and WHOOSH, was a quarter mile above the ground, blinking away the tears the wind had brought to her eyes. She wiped her cheeks with her buckskin sleeve, clearing her vision. From her vantage point, she counted fifteen dragons. She'd come well-armed for the assault, but her quiver only held twelve arrows. She pondered trying out the new weapons hanging on her belt, but with the dragons so far apart she wasn't certain the shrapnel would hit them efficiently. It would work better if they were close together, better still in an enclosed space.

Her sky-wall bow sang its musical ZING ZING ZING as she took out the three guards nearest the front door. As expected, the guards she'd left alive cried out the alarm. The remaining guards abandoned their posts to swarm to the front of the building to see what was going on.

Now it was time to use the new weapon. She freed one of the iron globes hanging from her belt. It was a bit larger than an apple and fairly heavy. Her father had called the device a grenade. She'd only had the afternoon to practice with them, but had been impressed by the damage they could do. Using them was simple. There was a ring at the top. She yanked it out swiftly, so that the attached flint would throw sparks. The grenade made a sizzling sound and gave off acrid smoke as the internal fuse burned. She threw it toward the cluster of guards. Unfortunately, a heavy iron ball thrown by hand didn't travel as swiftly as an arrow, even in a downward trajectory. She grimaced as the grenade exploded fifty feet above the clustered dragons. In the aftermath, a few clutched at injuries, but none had fallen. She frowned as shouts from countless dragons reached her. The bang and flash had to have alerted every dragon in town to the attack.

She cursed herself for choosing the novelty of the new weapon over the tried and true methods she knew best. Gritting her teeth, she willed herself into a dive. Half a second later, she pulled up inches from the ground ten feet in front of the guards. She willed her wings to fold against her back so they wouldn't be in her way, tossing aside her sky-wall bow to draw a longsword.

The dragons clustered in front of the door were so disorganized and distracted by the explosion overhead many were still looking up as she charged into them, conveniently exposing their throats. She killed four before the rest even fully understood there was an attacker right in front of their beaks. Not that the realization they were under attack did them any good. Earth-dragons were all brute force and heavy armor, with a fighting style even less graceful than Stonewall. But these muscle-bound, well-armored brutes had weak spots, and she knew these vulnerabilities well. Like a mother cat teaching its kittens how to hunt mice, at the age of five her father had taken her out to watch him ambush earth-dragons. Together, they would dissect the corpses until she knew earth-dragon anatomy far better than a biologian. Earth-dragon eyes were obvious weak spots, and beneath their boney beaks their windpipes and jugular veins weren't difficult to sever. Their powerful talons were useless once you cut the bulging tendons in their wrist, and their tree trunk legs mattered not at all once you severed the hamstrings.

It took her less than a minute to move among them. The attacks aimed at her were telegraphed and easily avoided, their battle-axes moving in slow motion arcs to her combat trained eyes. As the last one fell, she stood, panting, her heart racing, both from exertion and excitement. Though her father wasn't here, she could imagine him nodding at her in approval, which was usually the closest thing he ever gave her in the way of praise. But, since he wasn't here, she could at least take satisfaction that Stonewall had to have been impressed.

"That was the stupidest thing I've ever seen," grumbled Stonewall, dropping down from the sky beside her. "Charging into the center of them when you could have killed them all from safely above? Are you trying to get yourself killed?"

She had no time to respond to questions that were likely rhetorical anyway. There were footsteps on the other side of the door, and a familiar sizzling sound. She unfolded her wings and lunged at Stonewall, wrapping her arms around his chest. They shot straight up a hundred feet as the door flew open and a shotgun blast shook the night.

"We've found another gun," she said with a smirk, drawing a tomahawk from a sheath on her leg. She left Stonewall dangling in midair as she spun and planted the tomahawk between the eyes of the shotgun wielding dragon. Unfortunately, this proved to be an especially thick-skulled specimen. If the tomahawk jutting from his brow caused him any pain he didn't indicate it. He also proved adept at reloading, though even his relative speed was no match for Anza as she swooped down and snatched the gun away before he even finished pulling free the ramrod. She drove the butt of the gun into the earth-dragon's throat, and as the creature stumbled backward she pulled the ramrod free and took aim. She pulled the trigger and the fuse sizzled. Then... nothing. The gun failed to go off. She frowned, tossing the gun aside as she reached for her sword.

The gun went off as it struck the ground. She sucked in air as the lead balls tore into her left calf. If not for the support of the wings, she would have toppled over. The pain was blinding. Over the years she'd been stabbed, chopped, choked, bludgeoned and burned, but the shotgun blast was a new kind of injury, like being stabbed a dozen times at once while also being pounded on with hammers and burned with hot irons. She was caught so off balance by the pain that she didn't even see the earth-dragon tear free the tomahawk in its skull and brandish it, charging toward her.

Fortunately, Stonewall was ready. He slammed into her as he fell from the sky, knocking her aside, landing with his feet braced, mace in hand. The dragon swung the tomahawk but never really stood a chance. Stonewall swung his mace with both hands in a vicious blow dead to the center of the dragon's chest, knocking the beast back. The dragon landed on his back, crying in pain, the gurgling wetness of his voice signaling that something important in his chest was shattered.

Anza's head started to clear. The immediacy of the pain had caught her off guard, but any pain that lingered more than a few seconds she knew how to master. Her father had taught her strategies for dealing with pain, in lessons that to an outside observer would have looked like torture. She was grateful for the training as her mind carefully compartmentalized the pain. But pain wasn't her biggest problem. No amount of mental discipline was going to change the fact she was losing blood quickly.

Stonewall seemed to understand the danger as he grabbed her and they rose into the sky. They raced away from the rock house. He guided them to a large barn not far away, landing in the shadows behind it. He sat her on her feet and she immediately toppled, the left leg unable to bear any weight at all. He knelt over her and pulled off his shirt, tearing a long strip from it. In seconds, he had a tourniquet tightly twisted just below her knee. He produced a small canteen and poured water over her wound, frowning as he surveyed the damage. With a knife, he cut away the tattered buckskin of her pants leg, giving him a clear view of her mangled flesh.

"I've lived through worse," she said through clenched teeth, taking what was left of his shirt from him.

"You've severed an artery," he said. "All this blood—"

She started to wrap her leg tightly in long strips torn from his shirt. "You left the gun behind," she said.

"Saving your life seemed like a more immediate problem," he said.

"Saving my life wasn't the mission," she said, grimacing as the balls of lead still inside her calf burned even hotter as she increased the pressure. Her voice sounded very distant as she spoke. The night had a faint rumbling sound all around her, like the roar of a waterfall heard at a distance, but rhythmic, pulsing. She recognized it as the sound of her own blood struggling through her veins.

Whatever sounds she was hearing inside her, her new concerns were the sounds from the other side of the barn. Earth-dragons were shouting back and forth, accompanied by baying ox-dogs. Whatever element of surprise they'd possessed was lost.

Already, blood seeped through her bandages. She grabbed the handle of the dagger Stonewall had used to tighten the tourniquet and gave it another turn.

"If you choke off all the blood you might lose that leg," said Stonewall.

"Like father, like daughter," she said, grimly thinking of the injury that had taken her father's leg. She braced her hand against the barn and tried to stand, taking shallow, sharp breaths as tiny white stars danced in the air around her. Once she was standing, she willed herself a few inches off the ground, letting her wings take all the weight from her legs. Instantly, she felt the pain and pressure lessen. It helped also that the extra turn of the tourniquet had choked off deep nerves, helping her leg grow numb.

"Will you be able to fly back to Dragon Forge on your own?" he asked.

"Once we've gotten what we came for."

"You can't keep fighting with an injury like this."

She patted the grenades on her belt. "With these I can." Without further argument, she rose high above the village, though not too high. She'd learned her lesson about the distance the grenades could travel before going off.

They'd apparently been spotted when they flew behind the barn because a gang of earth-dragons headed toward it, with a trio of leashed ox-dogs baying before them. Of all the things she'd killed over the years, only ox-dogs gave her any twinge of remorse. They were only doing what they'd been trained to do, so she felt a bit of kinship with them. She dropped two sputtering grenades into the thick of the mob. There were stark shadows and thunderous noise and utter chaos followed as dragons fled in all directions, leaving behind a dead ox-dog and half a dozen fallen companions.

Satisfied with her tactic, she flew toward the rock house, where another cluster of earth-dragons stood around the door, at least thirty of them. This time she dropped three grenades in rapid succession and gave a grim smile at the effectiveness of the tactic.

"If you'd done this the first time instead of charging into the thick of things you wouldn't have gotten hurt," said Stonewall, coming up beside her in the sky.

"Why do you feel this is an appropriate time for a scolding?" asked Anza.

"By my count, I've saved your life twice already," said Stonewall. "Let's try not to test my reflexes again."

"I'm only counting once," said Anza. "Months ago, when Vulpine tore off my wings."

"And tonight when—"

"I would have gotten out of the way," she said. "Besides, I flew you out of the path of a shotgun blast, so we're even."

Stonewall nodded. "That's true. How did you know he was about to throw open the door and shoot at us?"

"I pay attention," she said. "You should try it some time."

Stonewall laughed. She cocked her head, mystified by his reaction.

He gave a shrug and said, "No one ever talks back to me. Because of my size, people go out of their way to be polite. I find your attitude refreshing."

"No one ever talks back to me either," she said.

"You do have a reputation as being quick to draw a blade. But I know you well enough to know you only do when someone actually deserves it."

"If we're done with our mutual admiration, perhaps we should go get the guns?" she asked.

Stonewall grinned. "I don't think I'm done admiring you by a long shot, but let's do this." He pulled his sky-wall bow and quiver from his back and held them toward her. "This time, I take the lead. Stay out of reach and take out as many dragons as you can from up here."

"Agreed," she said, taking the bow, though at the moment there was no one to target. Any dragons inside the rock house were apparently smart enough not to come out after witnessing fire and destruction rain from the sky. Assuming there were any dragons left inside. The front door stood wide open.

Stonewall flew down beside the door, his wings folding behind him as he pressed his back to the wall, listening for any sounds within. Apparently, he heard something, since he tightened his grip on his mace as his whole body tensed. With a burst of speed, he slipped into the room, out of Anza's sight. There was a loud *CRASH* and a hard *THUMP*, followed by dragons crying out in distress.

More importantly, it was followed by a rectangle of light as the backdoor of the house flew open. Someone was making his escape. She could see the shadow of an earth-dragon cast out over the overgrown rear lawn. Curiously, she couldn't see an actual dragon, even though the shadow indicated someone was now charging outside. The high grass and brambles began to be trampled, as if an invisible being were moving across them at a high rate of speed.

No. Not invisible. Camouflaged. Bigmouth had the chameleon mutation that allowed him to blend into his background. In the dim light this ability would be especially effective, but near the house his shadow betrayed him.

He obviously wasn't carrying any guns, or anything at all for that matter, since the chameleon effect couldn't hide weaponry and armor. Black Silence assassins often fought with slender ebony blades that were easily concealed, but the shadow didn't reveal such a weapon. Apparently, Bigmouth was only concerned with escape.

Since he was still the dragon most likely to know the location of any remaining guns, lobbing a grenade at Bigmouth wasn't an option. She steadied her bow, using the moving shadows to aim for her concealed foe's legs. Hitting an unseen target in headlong flight would have been less of a challenge if she wasn't a bit lightheaded from her blood loss, but at least an earth-dragon was a fair-sized target.

She released her arrow, the sky-wall bow ringing out with its characteristic ZING! This proved to be a wasted arrow, as it punched into the ground mere inches behind the source of the fleeing shadow, failing to connect. The shadow paused, plainly hearing something that hinted at danger, but not yet having figured out where the attack was coming from. She aimed her second shot. Now that Bigmouth had paused, she was certain she could put an arrow into his thigh. Certainty turned to consternation as she released the arrow and the dragon's shadow head jerked up. The sound of the bow traveled faster than the arrow, and dragons with the chameleon mutation were also gifted with superior reflexes. The dragon leapt backward as her second arrow punched into the ground where he'd stood.

Bigmouth's shadow showed him looking at the sky. Despite the darkness and the general poor vision of earth-dragons, her wings must have betrayed her, because his shadow indicated he was now looking right at her.

Fine. Let him see the next arrow she fired. She aimed it slightly in front of where he stood, certain he would leap backward to avoid it, and a fraction of a second later she released a second arrow, aiming where she expected him to land when he dodged the first. But he defied expectations, diving forward, rolling fluidly back to his feet, and darting into the deep shadows spreading from the corner of the rock house.

In growing frustration, she fired two more arrows, three, four, five, no longer aiming for his legs, targeting where she thought his center mass would be. None found their target. She growled as she reached back to the quiver and found only a single arrow left. She imagined the stern look in her father's eyes when he learned how badly she'd botched such a simple task. She put the final arrow against the string, knowing she now had literally one last shot at redemption.

Bigmouth had reached the shadows and couldn't be seen at all. She couldn't let him escape, and now that he was aware of her he wouldn't be foolish enough to let himself cast more shadows. He also had to know that, from her vantage point, she'd notice if he recklessly crashed through brush or grass. But, from high above, she might never hear if he simply walked away slowly, taking care with his path.

Despite the risk, she had to go to the ground. Yes, he was fast, but at close range she would be faster. While a hundred feet was more than enough space for an attentive foe to dodge an arrow, at point blank even fast reflexes wouldn't let something the size of an earth-dragon get out of the way.

She dropped into the shadow at the corner of the house, about thirty feet out, listening closely, her arrow nocked, the bow drawn. Unlike a longbow, the pulleys of a sky-wall bow allowed her to hold a drawn arrow for as long as she needed without feeling strain. She would make this arrow count, assuming he was still there.

Which, she realized, he was. She could hear him breathing. His acrobatics in avoiding her arrows had winded him. He was very close to the wall, catching his breath, standing perfectly still, waiting. Her brow furrowed as she studied the darkness, looking for any tiny glint of light that might reflect from his eyes, or the faintest change in the density of the shadows that might show his limbs or torso.

"I see you," she said, bluffing. "Surrender and I'll spare you."

"How generous," said Bigmouth.

She released the arrow, pinpointing his location by his voice.

The shadows moved. The arrow stopped a foot from the wall, seeming to hang in mid-air. She thought she'd hit him, until Bigmouth chuckled.

Anza's mouth dropped open slowly as she realized he'd caught the arrow.

The arrow moved toward her, still in her unseen foe's grasp. She floated back a step, drawing her sword.

"You must know little about the training we go through to join the Black Silence," said Bigmouth. "Our masters routinely shoot at us with bows. If we don't learn to dodge, we die. Eventually, they bind our legs. To survive, we learn to catch. You never stood a chance."

"I see things differently," she said, unimpressed by his boasting. He'd fled the house to avoid danger. His courage was nothing but bluster. "I have a sword. You're unarmed."

Bigmouth chuckled again. "I've already slipped the caps off my poisoned claws. You'd already be dead if I wanted you dead. Lucky for you, I know who you are."

Anza said nothing, still straining her eyes to make sense of the seemingly formless shadows before her. Only the arrow he held showed the precise location of his arm. She couldn't even be certain if he held it in his right talon or his left. The combination of chameleon shading and deep shadows was more than even her keen eyes could decipher.

"They call you Anza," said Bigmouth. "You're Burke's daughter. He's the genius behind these new weapons you humans have been so proud of. I can't believe he was so stupid to send his own flesh and blood into my grasp. You're a prize of immeasurable value."

The arrow moved toward her another step. She tensed, raising her sword.

"Do you wonder how I know so much about you?" asked Bigmouth. "Burke might be a genius, but he's surrounded by men who'd sell out their own mothers for a jug of whiskey. Men who your father has entrusted with secrets reveal all once their tongues are loosened by drink. And once I learn their secrets, all men can be controlled with the right incentives. Just as your father will no doubt prove cooperative should he wish to see you ag—"

Anza struck. The night before, she'd been goaded into attacking by Bitterwood and as a result had lost the element of surprise. Bigmouth perhaps was attempting the same tactic, but unlike the confrontation with Bitterwood, she now had wings. Her normal attack speed was something few foes could counter, but with his arrow-catching swiftness, Bigmouth was likely her match. What he couldn't know was that her wings could carry her far swifter than an arrow. With her sword held before her gripped in both hands, she grunted as she drove the tip into his shoulder, driving through to the hilt, her momentum knocking Bigmouth backward even though the muscular earth-dragon outweighed her by two-hundred pounds or more. Her blade bent against the rock wall behind him and she drove her forearm hard into his throat for a final push, bashing his head into the stone. She immediately flitted backward, reaching for her tomahawks as Bigmouth rebounded from the wall, flailing wildly as he slashed the air before him with his poisoned claws, then sank to his knees.

With a groan, he grabbed the blade in his shoulder and pulled, but the bent blade refused to draw free. He breathed heavily, but rhythmically. Anza knew the sound well. It was the way her own breath sounded as she shut off her own pain.

"We've much in common," she said. "I, too, am well versed in the art of poison. The compound that coats my blade will kill you in moments, but there is an antidote. Tell me everything you know about the location of the guns and perhaps I'll give it to you."

"You're bluffing," Bigmouth said.

"And you're bleeding," she said. "The poison is nearly irrelevant. You'll bleed out before it takes hold."

"Fah," said Bigmouth, shaking his head. "This scratch?" He rose to his feet. His left arm hung limp but he held his right talon in a menacing pose, the claws like sharp spikes.

Anza carefully rose a few yards higher, far beyond any distance he could possibly jump. Bigmouth's skin had settled into a uniform deep green, almost black, still difficult to see, but not impossible. Perhaps pain prevented him from employing his camouflage, or perhaps he no longer worried about hiding himself since the blade jutting from his shoulder would be visible, and his blood spilling on the ground would mark any path he might use to flee.

Or might there be another reason he chose to be seen? His eyes. They weren't really fixed upon her, but gazed at the sky beyond. What if he remained visible because he wanted to hold her attention?

She spun around, confirming her suspicions. A trio of sky-dragons approached her in the dark sky, gliding in utter silence, the closest perhaps twenty yards away. The glint of iron helmets revealed these to be valkyries. Each carried a long spear in her hind talons. The nearest rose swiftly, throwing her spear at the center of Anza's chest. But Bigmouth wasn't the only combatant trained in handling missiles. She slashed out with her tomahawk with perfect timing, striking the spear point when it was only arm's length from impact, knocking it aside. Unfortunately, she'd never performed this maneuver wearing wings. The deflected spear punched through the thin metal of her left wing with a sound that made the metal cry out like a shriek. In the aftermath, the hole threw sparks and the smell of hot metal reached Anza's nostrils. Then, despite her willing the wings to carry her swiftly higher, she started to slowly drop toward the ground. She'd experienced this before; even the slightest damage to the wings would remove them from her control and carry her gently to earth. She was a sitting duck as a second valkyrie flew straight at her, holding her spear tightly in her hind-talons, seemingly intent on driving it straight through Anza's heart with her full momentum.

Anza reached behind her and grabbed the edge of a wing. With a grunt she tore free of the silver disk adhered to her back. She dropped, no more than ten feet off the ground, as the valkyrie slammed into the still floating wings with a sound like clashing cymbals.

In almost any other circumstance, a ten foot drop would have been easily managed. Stay loose, keep her knees bent, roll forward, and spring back to her feet. Unfortunately, with her mangled leg, the long practiced motion proved less than graceful. The pain was like white hot lightning flashing through her skull. She rolled forward, but instead of springing to her feet wound up on her hands and knees, sucking air, fighting to clear her head.

She heard the flap of a sky-dragon's wings and raised up on her knees, as a valkyrie raced toward her. Without thought, through muscle memory alone, Anza hurled her tomahawk and buried the blade directly between the valkyrie's eyes. The sky-dragon turned into a hurtling sack of meat, hitting the ground a yard in front of Anza, tumbling limply toward her. Anza fell to her side, avoiding the worst of the sky-dragon's mass, but had no way of avoiding the seemingly endless blanket of the wing that fell over her. She kicked and clawed to pull herself free, reaching open air, looking up at the last second as a shadow fell over the edge of her hand.

Above her stood Bigmouth, carrying the spear that had punched through her wing. With a grunt, he drove the butt-end of the shaft into the back of her skull, and Anza's world went dark and quiet.

SHE WOKE as she was trained to wake, silent, still, her eyes closed, offering no hint that her unconsciousness had passed. She kept her breathing steady as she let her senses expand. She didn't need her eyes to gain a wealth of information about her surroundings.

First, her wrists were bound behind her. The itching of her wrists told her she was only held with hemp rope. Second, her belt had been removed, as well as all of the sheaths and holsters strapped to her legs and upper arms that held her small armory of blades. However, she was still dressed. The dragons probably had no clue that the buttons on the front of her buckskin vest concealed tiny razor disks. Nor had they removed the small, seemingly innocuous steel ring she wore on the middle finger of her right hand.

She was on a wooden floor, covered with grit and grime. The wooden planks carried the creak and shuffle of everyone in the room currently on their feet. Most were dragons. She could hear the clicking of claws distinctly enough. But there was also a softer tread, a human in boots.

Then the human spoke, in a voice she knew well. *Thorny.*

"I wish I could tell you Burke would give in," said Thorny. "But, no matter what you've heard, Anza's not really his daughter. He's not going to give up Dragon Forge to save her."

"Then why should we keep her alive?" asked a sky-dragon, female, a valkyrie. "She killed Kysette in front of our eyes. That she's still breathing is an insult."

"You're looking at this all wrong," said Thorny. "Look, I've known Burke for damn near twenty years. He thinks I'm a friend, but he doesn't have a clue what friendship is. The way he orders me around, expects me to do stuff without even a thank you, it's kind of like I'm a slave, only he doesn't even have to feed and clothe me."

"Or give you whiskey," said a deep voice. It was Bigmouth. If he was feeling any weakness from his injury he hid it well. It was a shame she'd been bluffing about the poison.

"All I'm saying," said Thorny, "is that Burke has never thought of me as an equal. While he expects me to run errands and occasionally help organize his papers, he's never treated me as a confidant. He doesn't trust me enough to tell me how he makes gunpowder, but Anza might know. She's by his side more than anyone."

Even though only Thorny, the valkyrie, and Bigmouth had spoken, they weren't the only ones present. There were at least five earth-dragons, and a second valkyrie. But she could also tell there was one more human in the room, someone big, his breathing steady, resting on the floor beside her. She inhaled deeply, though carefully, still not letting on she was awake. The smell confirmed what she'd guessed. Beneath the stink of dragons, and the boozy aura that permeated any room Thorny stood in, she smelled the sweat of a man who'd fought hard earlier, a scent she recognized. Stonewall was also a captive.

"Then let's rephrase the question," said the valkyrie, responding to Thorny. "If this girl knows all you say she knows, why do we need you?"

"I'm the best spy Bigmouth has," said Thorny.

"Or perhaps the best spy Burke has," said the valkyrie.

"You don't think I haven't thought of that?" asked Bigmouth, sounding a little insulted. "Of course he's spying for Burke. He confessed it all the first night I met him, once I got him drunk enough. This makes him the perfect tool for feeding Burke whatever lies I want him to believe. At this point, Thorny's in so deep he's got no choice but to do anything I tell him. The humans would string him up like a pig if they found out the truth."

"You don't need threats to make me hate Burke," said Thorny. "Look at my hands. For twenty years he's bossed me around, making me build stuff for him. I must have hammered in half the nails that held together that damned tavern of his. I'd tell him I needed to rest and he'd just cuss at me until I worked harder. He ruined my damned hands. I owe that bastard nothing."

"You expect us to believe you'd betray all mankind?" said the valkyrie.

"Have you met mankind?" asked Thorny.

"I still say we kill him," said the valkyrie, sounding as if she'd turned toward Bigmouth. "We should tie up loose ends. Kill the man and the girl as well. Let it be a mystery as long as it can what has happened to them and to the weapons. We've created a secure shelter at the Nest for a team of biologians to figure out how these guns function. Vulpine made a serious error in taking the last captured gun to the College of Spires. No one can possibly recover the guns from the Nest. Still, the more time we give the biologians to figure out how these items work, the better."

"I can tell you how they work," said Bigmouth. "My enforcers have experimented with the shotguns. We can load and fire them easily enough."

"Can you make more gunpowder?"

"No."

"And now there are these new mysteries," said a second sky-dragon, another valkyrie, sounding as if she was on the far side of the room. "These wings the humans wore. How can they possibly function? We heard reports that winged humans had been seen during Vulpine's seige of Dragon Forge but gave the rumors little credit. If humans can now fly—"

"Not many of us," said Thorny. "We've only got a few sets of the wings. They're old technology, from the Human Age, we think. Most of 'em have stopped working, and Burke can't fix 'em, since we don't know why they worked in the first place."

"I'm more interested in how those iron spheres do so much damage," said Bigmouth. "With a hundred of these, a squad of valkyries flying above the range of a sky-wall bow could make short work of any human resistance."

"I can tell you how they work," said Thorny.

"Stop!" barked the valkyrie.

Anza cracked her eyes, knowing that whatever Thorny was doing, everyone in the room would be looking at him.

Thorny stood next to a heavy wooden table. He was guarded by two earth-dragons who stood on either side of him, battle-axes at the ready, looking prepared to lop off his head if Bigmouth gave the word. Bigmouth stood on the opposite side of the table, next to a valkyrie, the one who had thrown her spear at Anza. Other earth-dragons were scattered around the room, and the second valkyrie stood next to the door, a spear held in her fore-talons.

Thorny's gnarled hand was stretched before him, motionless over something on the table Anza couldn't see from the floor. She suspected the table must have held at least one grenade, and perhaps her whole arsenal.

Thorny cleared his throat. "I'm not gonna do anything stupid. I want to show you how you work one of the grenades. They're really easy once you know the trick."

"Trick?" asked Bigmouth.

"Yeah," said Thorny. "I mean, you saw the damage these things can do. You can't just run around with them primed. You've got to load 'em up with powder at the last second."

"Load them how?" asked Bigmouth.

"You unscrew that knob at the top. But you can't make it turn until you pull out that pin. It's a safety feature."

"Show me," said Bigmouth, picking up the grenade and handing it to Thorny. Anza noted that Bigmouth's movements were stiff. His wounded shoulder had been bandaged, but it obviously still caused him pain. Her own injury could no longer be felt. Her leg below the tourniquet was completely numb.

The valkyrie practically choked on her own spit as Thorny took the grenade, making a yawping noise as she thrust out her fore-talon and snatched the grenade away. "Are you insane? He'll kill us all!"

"What? And kill himself?" asked Bigmouth, with an amused glint in his eyes. "You plainly know nothing about the survival instincts of men. You valkyries can go your whole life without meeting a human since you don't allow slaves in the Nest."

"Unlike earth-dragons, sky-dragons value their young," said the valkyrie. "Letting a human near the fledglings would be like a human inviting wolves to stand guard over their cradles."

"You fear men because you don't understand them," said Bigmouth. "Whereas I know them well enough that I'm building an empire directly beneath Burke's nose, with money, supplies, and weapons willingly given to me by his own men."

"You trust men too much," said the valkyrie.

"I trust them not at all," said Bigmouth. "I master them. Your analogy with the wolves and cradles shows a woeful ignorance of the way the world truly works. Men long ago tamed wolves. The once wild beasts willingly stand guard over infants, and slobber gratefully over the tiniest morsels of praise given to them. So it is with men. A thousand years of slavery have bred out their willfulness. Thorny's too tame to betray me. He's a dog, clever enough to walk on two legs. He knows that, if he pleases me, there will be a new jug of whiskey for a reward. You do like your whisky, don't you Thorny?"

"Yes sir," said Thorny, casting his eyes downward.

"Give him the grenade," said Bigmouth, fixing his gaze on the valkyrie.

The valkyrie narrowed her eyes and looked for a moment as if she might go for Bigmouth's throat. A long second passed, then another, and finally she handed Thorny the globe.

"You gotta do this just right," said Thorny. "Lean in close."

The valkyrie and Bigmouth leaned in. Thorny held the grenade in one twisted hand as he hooked a bony finger through the loop of wire at the end of the pin. "Step one, you pull this out."

He pulled the pin free. The grenade sizzled, giving off smoke. "Woof," said Thorny, as a grin played across his grizzled face.

Anza pushed the ring from her finger into her palm and twisted it once. The ring was formed by two interlocking bands. Twisting one band against the other caused a tiny blade to emerge from a groove. She sawed at the ropes that bound her wrist, though there was no way she would sever them before the grenade exploded.

To her shock, Stonewall proved to be as awake and alert as she was. He suddenly rolled from where he lay on his back to rest on top of her, crushing her with his bulk, his body a barrier between her and the grenade.

The explosion in the confined space was deafening. Anza squirmed, slipping from under Stonewall, her leg, numb only seconds ago, suddenly angry and jangling with each movement. She looked over the room as she sliced through hemp strands one by one. A few of the earth-dragons on the farther reaches of the room were stumbling around, dazed and bleeding. There were several bodies on the floor, including the valkyrie who'd been near the table. The table had been sturdy, built of oak planks, but she was surprised to see it standing, though it couldn't be described as intact. It looked as if someone had taken out their frustrations on it with an ax.

But the thing that most caught her eye was the final valkyrie. She was bleeding from her neck as she bent down to pick up something from the floor. When she straightened again, she was holding an unexploded grenade, as well as a ranger's belt, which still had the gunpowder pouch attached to it. The valkyrie looked around the room once more, her eyes lingering on the form of her fallen sister for only a few seconds, then she opened the door and moved out into the night.

Anza felt the hemp growing slack as strands peeled away. Straining with all her strength she snapped the rope. She rose, bracing herself against the wall, her injured leg feeling as if it was actively being chewed on my some unseen, toothy beast.

Stonewall had also survived the blast. The oak table had caught most of the shrapnel from the bottom half of the exploding grenade, making the floor the safest place in the room. Stonewall rolled over and sat up, the muscles in his shoulders and neck bulging as he expended all the pressure he could against the ropes that bound his arms. The hemp twisted and stretched under the pressure, but didn't break. It did, however, create enough slack that Stonewall could wriggle free. He rose on trembling legs. His bare back was covered with blood, but as the blood flowed away she saw the blood wasn't his own. Not that he was free from injury. He had a huge knot on the side of his temple and his left eye was purple and swollen shut. His lower lip was split, making his words slightly slurred as he said, "You alright?"

"No," she said, limping along the wall toward the door. She stopped when she saw what was left of Thorny. Both arms below the elbow were gone, and his chest was bleeding from innumerable wounds. To her horror, she saw he was still alive, conscious of his fate as he stared up, blinking, his lips moving slowly.

She dropped to her knees despite the pain. "Thorny!" she said, placing her hand on his shoulder.

"Your... wings..." he wheezed. "On... the table..."

"Don't speak," she said. "I'll... we'll get you... you'll..." She swallowed hard, words failing her.

Thorny shook his head. "It's... fine." Then he closed his eyes and went completely still.

"No," whispered Anza.

But she had no time to mourn, because at that second she saw one of the wing disks rise from the cluttered floor, seemingly levitating on its own. With a second glance, she saw the truth. Bigmouth was still alive, his camouflage powers engaged, his position betrayed by his bandaged shoulder and the wing disk. With his extraordinary reflexes, he must have ducked under the table before the grenade exploded. But, at ground zero, the blast couldn't have done his ears any good, and Bigmouth didn't react as Stonewall charged him from behind, both fists raised, then bashed him in the back of the skull, dropping him.

Stonewall snatched up the disk and shouted, "I'm going after the valkyrie!"

"Hurry!" said Anza, once more fighting to get back on her feet.

By now, most of the remaining earth-dragons not killed by the blast had stumbled outside, but one had the sense of mind to place himself in the doorway, battle-axe held at the ready, eyes focused on Stonewall.

Anza glanced around the clutter of the floor. Apparently all their weapons and gear had been in the room. Her heart leapt as she caught a glimpse of silver beneath the edge of the fallen valkyrie. The second wing disk! And of even more immediate utility, she spotted what was left of her own belt, and the throwing knives it held. She leapt toward the belt, though in her present condition there was little difference between leaping and falling. With arms outstretched, she closed her fingers around the belt.

Stonewall, meanwhile, had wisely chosen not to attack the earth-dragon unarmed and had picked up the fallen valkyrie's spear, looking ready to charge the door. Anza rolled into a sitting position. She had no doubt Stonewall could outfight the dragon in the doorway, but saw no need for him to waste time doing so. The dragon made no effort to dodge as she hurled a throwing knife. A heartbeat later and the dragon was on his back, the blade sunk to the hilt in his eye socket.

"Go!" she called to Stonewall, clenching her teeth as she crawled toward her own disk.

Stonewall went, slapping the wing disk on his back as he raced through the door. Once in the open air, his wings unfolded with a wind chime melody. He leapt into the sky and never came down.

Anza reached the second wing disk. Assuming this was the one she'd been wearing, she hoped that it was finished repairing itself. In practicing with them, she'd pushed her skills and more than once clipped her wings against branches or walls, so she'd experienced the sensation of the wings kicking into their safety mode before. She also learned that whoever had made the wings had designed them to repair themselves. She wasn't certain how much time had passed, but hoped that the wings would once again carry her.

She glanced at her injured leg. The bandage was brown with dried blood. The tourniquet had lost all tension because the dragons had removed the dagger that had been used to tighten it. Blood was flowing into the leg once more. Since she wasn't still losing blood, her wounds had likely clotted beneath the bandages. If she engaged in too much activity she would probably start bleeding again. She doubted she had much blood to spare. The prudent thing to do would be to fly back to Dragon Forge and trust that Stonewall would overtake the valkyrie.

But Thorny hadn't died bravely for her to flee like a coward. The mission still mattered more than her life.

She put the disk on her back. There was no room to open the wings inside, so she still had to rely on her own legs to get out of the room. Fortunately, she could use the table for support. Equally fortunate, as she rose, she spotted her tomahawk among the rubble. She picked it up. The leather binding of the handle was torn by shrapnel, but the cutting edge of the head was still razor sharp. She hopped to the door, her eyes spotting fragments of guns scattered across the room. Most had been on the table when the grenade went off, and were now shattered and twisted. Then, luck delivered another gift, a single grenade still intact, resting against the wall. She groaned as she knelt to retrieve it. Finally, she made it to the door, hopped into the night air, and found herself surrounded by a mob of earth-dragons who'd gathered outside to find out what all the commotion was about.

Anza stared at the earth-dragons in silent contempt as they looked her over in confusion. One by one, she could see light flickering in their eyes that she might, possibly, be someone they were supposed to kill. A few of them lifted their battle-axes, looking ready to charge.

Anza said, "Catch," as she pulled the pin from the grenade. She tossed it to the closest earth-dragon. He caught it.

This would be a very bad time to find out that her wings hadn't finished repairing themselves, she thought. With a second thought, she unfolded the wings, and with a third she shot into the sky, and was a hundred yards above when the grenade finally released the fire and death within it.

She kept climbing, until the town beneath her was only a few small specks from lanterns and she no longer heard the shouts of earth-dragons. To the south, Dragon Forge glowed a hellish red, the light of countless lanterns reflecting from the smoke of the never-cooling foundries, the fart-stink of coal tainting the wind even though she was ten miles away. Off to the west, there was a faint glow on the horizon marking the location of the Nest. The silver ribbon of the winding river that connected the Nest and Dragon Forge glinted here and there through gaps in trees. With her wings, she would be faster than a valkyrie, but sky-dragons were still swift enough that she had less than an hour to find and kill her target. If the valkyrie reached the Nest, all was lost. Even in perfect health, she doubted she could penetrate far into that heavily guarded den of trained warriors.

Of course, the fact that she could see the lights of the Nest, even dimly, meant she knew precisely where her target was heading. Even though she couldn't see the sky-dragon or Stonewall, she knew the direction they would be flying.

She paused a moment more, confident the speed of her wings would carry her the needed distance in time, but far less confident her mind was clear and focused enough to do what must be done. She closed her eyes and inhaled deeply, trying to once again box in the pain in her leg.

This proved to be a mistake. With her eyes closed, horrors spilled across the blank canvas of her mind. She could see Thorny clear as day, his arms mere stumps, his life spilling away with each heartbeat. She'd known Thorny her whole life; she'd called him uncle, though there was no blood relation between them. Her father had always treated her like a machine to be fine-tuned, had worked tirelessly to sharpen her mind and harden her body and to extinguish any capacity for fear or doubt or hesitation against a more fearsome foe. His idea of a father/daughter outing was to lurk among the trees of the Forge Road far from town and wait for a band of earth-dragons to pass, to offer her the faintest praise when she killed them all, alone, then to criticize her while she was still warm with pride, pointing out every close call, every missed opportunity, and every wasted motion that could have been avoided to accomplish her mission more swiftly and with less risk. His birthday gifts to her had been knives and swords and war paint.

If not for Thorny, she might never have tasted a piece of candy. If not for Thorny, she might never have laughed at stupid, silly jokes, or learned the words to childish songs, even if she couldn't sing them. When every other person in the town of Burke's Tavern had looked upon her with either fear or scorn, Thorny alone never failed to greet her with a smile and a hug.

What had her father been thinking to send an old man, barely able to use his hands, into the thick of their greatest enemies? Thorny was his best friend, perhaps his only friend. Why put him in such danger? Of course, she knew the answer. Getting information from Multon was a problem and Thorny was a tool perfectly crafted to solve that problem.

She sometimes wondered, in her father's eyes, if people even existed. With his analytical approach to the world, he seemed to see everyone as mere gears in the vast machinery of life. He might appreciate each gear for its function in turning the wheels of the world, but, as a mechanic, he felt no great loss in tossing aside a worn gear and replacing it with another.

She clenched her fists tightly, fighting to clear her mind. What was the use of such musings? How had they wormed their way into her brain? They were cancerous, diseased thoughts. They would kill her if she let them grow. She closed her eyes again. This time, she allowed no idle thoughts. In seconds, with careful breathing, the pain of Thorny's death had been pushed into the same cage as the agony in her leg. She closed the door on both and opened her eyes, clear-headed and free of hurt.

Ahead, unseen in the dark, flew a dragon she must kill.

She took a deep breath, held it, and willed herself in the direction of the Nest. The wind pounded her mercilessly, an invisible waterfall that would have crushed her if she hadn't practiced how to hold her arms before her as if in a dive, aiming her body like an arrow to give as little surface as possible to the air. In seconds she traveled miles, then slowed, breathing again, searching for any hint of... there! Not the valkyrie, but a flash of silver, and the shadow of a man flying over trees. She flew down to him and called out, "Stonewall!"

He looked toward her and said, "I told you I'd handle this! You're injured!"

"Have you looked at your face?" she asked. "You can only open one eye."

He nodded. "And that's not doing me any good. I haven't seen any hint of the valkyrie. There are a thousand places she might have found cover along the way, dropping down below the treetops. I don't see how we'll ever find her if she's hiding."

Anza pressed her lips together tightly as she pondered this. He was right, the valkyrie could hide, but instinctively it made no sense. No sky-dragon would willingly travel the distance back to the Nest over ground, and why bother hiding during the night when you would be far more visible during the day? Besides, the valkyrie had fled before Stonewall had recovered his wings. The valkyrie couldn't be certain she was being pursued. No, she had to be heading for the Nest. So why couldn't she be spotted? It was dark, yes, with the moon only a sliver, but it was cloudless, and, unlike Bigmouth, this dragon couldn't camouflage herself.

But she didn't need to camouflage herself. In the moonlight, the thick canopy of the forest was an undulating surface of irregular shadows, a nearly impossible backdrop to spot something against, if you were looking down upon it. Anza had been flying high, since instinct told her that the higher she was, the more she could see. In retrospect, this was entirely the wrong strategy.

"Follow me," said Anza, flying in the direction of the Nest, though aiming slightly to the north. Stonewall followed. She stopped moving and turned back in the direction of Dragon Forge, which still glowed in the distance. She dropped lower and lower toward the trees, until her toes brushed against the highest branches.

There, against the glow of the town, she spotted her target. Unfortunately, she found too many targets. The silhouettes of at least ten sky-dragons flapped low above the trees.

"See anything?" asked Stonewall, floating beside her.

"You don't?" she asked.

"I am down to one eye," he said. "Truth be told, my vision is still kind of hazy. Those dragons knocked me pretty good with the butt of an axe. I've got no idea how long I was out. I'm lucky they didn't cut my damned throat."

"Bigmouth thought I'd be useful for blackmail," said Anza. "He probably recognized you as well, and figured that the captain of the rangers would be worth more alive than dead."

"How would he even recognize me?" asked Stonewall.

"You are, you know, pretty much the biggest person anyone's ever laid eyes on."

"One day you'll have to meet my older brother," said Stonewall. "I'm a runt next to him."

"Anyway, yes, I see something," said Anza, returning to the mission at hand. "A lot of somethings. At least ten valkyrie. There must have been more waiting somewhere in the town or along the river."

"Those aren't great odds," said Stonewall.

"I've faced worse," said Anza. "The most dragons I've killed in a single fight was fifty-seven."

"No wonder everyone's scared of you back at the fort."

"Everyone?"

"Well, not everyone," he said, with a grin. "I found you a little hard to figure out at first, I admit. I wasn't comfortable with the idea of Burke sending a woman into battle, especially not his own daughter. But, I guess that's one reason Burke's a genius and I'm not. Burke told me all about how you infiltrated the College of Spires by yourself to retrieve the gun Vulpine stole. You obviously have the fighting skills to handle anything. More than that, you've got grit."

"Grit?"

"Courage. Character. It's a good thing."

"Grit," she said. "I like your grit as well."

"Why don't we show these valkyries that they don't own these skies?" he asked.

"Agreed. Let's go high. They might not have spotted us yet. Sky-dragons have better vision than most humans, but they don't have eyes in the top of their heads. I'll get us positioned above them, and trust that once we get within a hundred feet or so you'll be able to see them even with your impaired vision. They look like they're flying in formation, probably a diamond shape with one guarded in the middle. I'll aim for the center, you take out the one on point. We don't need to fight them all. Once we find the one with the grenade and the gunpowder and retrieve those, we turn tail and head back to Dragon Forge at top speed. The air might be their natural element, but these wings give us an edge."

Stonewall gave her the thumbs up. "I'll follow your lead."

Anza nodded, turning her face toward the skies, rising rapidly. The constellations were spread before her in a dazzling array. The smoke of Dragon Forge normally blotted out all but the brightest planets, but this far out from the city she could faintly make out the milky band of pale light that spilled across the heavens. She hung still for a moment, drinking in the starlight, clearing her mind of all thoughts save for the coming battle.

"It's beautiful up here," said Stonewall, breaking the silence.

It was the sort of small, pointless observation she found tiring when spoken by others. But, from his lips, she, too, became aware of the beauty, until a voice within her reminded her of how foolish it was to waste time contemplating such things.

"My father would disagree," said Anza. "He says the stars above are distant suns, so far away many have already burned out, but only now is the light reaching us. He says the only useful purpose of the stars it measuring time and marking latitude. Beyond this, they only serve to remind us of how insignificant we are in the vastness of time and space."

"Your father's not one for poetry or art, I take it," said Stonewall.

"Ah, but you're wrong," she said, fixing hard eyes upon him. "I am his sculpture. I am his song of death."

And with that, she zoomed off. Any human weakness inside her was squelched into nothingness as the clockwork of her mind and muscles took over, turning her once more into a finely tuned battle engine.

She flashed from the sky like lightning, holding the tomahawk in her right hand. Below her the dragons flew much as she'd guessed, in a diamond formation, with four at the outer points of the diamond, four balanced at the midpoints of the edges of the diamond, and two protected in the center. Her instinct said to attack the rear one, so she slowed her dive mere feet above her target and dropped onto the dragon's back like a wildcat. The dragon had no time to call out in alarm before Anza leaned forward and used the razor edge of the tomahawk to cut the creature's throat. Instantly the dragon fell away, tumbling, her spear falling beside her. She searched for any sign of the grenade or powder pouch, and frown as she realized she'd picked the wrong target.

At that second, Stonewall hit the lead dragon, driving his spear deep into her spine. The dragon fell away, tearing the embedded spear from Stonewall's grasp, leaving him unarmed. Instantly, the two dragons on either side of the diamond point veered toward him. The one to his right threw her spear and he darted from its path, but with his swollen eye he failed to see the one approach from his left and hurl her spear.

Anza raced forward, hand outstretched, and caught the spear mere inches from his side. She instantly spun around and threw the spear back at the valkyrie who'd attacked. The sky-dragon was rising in the aftermath of her throw, wearing the traditional light armor that protected her torso, but no armor yet designed could protect her wings. The spear tore into the left wing and dangled there. The valkyrie squawked as she went into a rapid spiral toward the trees below.

Anza had no time to see if the dragon survived her fall, since she and Stonewall were now the targets of a barrage of spears. The heat of combat had speeded her perceptions and she tracked each spear with ease, flitting above the barrage and targeting the nearest valkyrie with one of her throwing knives. The blade sank into the dragon's shoulder and the valkyrie dropped, one wing useless, the other spread to turn her into a whirling pinwheel as she fell.

Behind her, Stonewall cried out in pain. She turned to find a dragon on his back, her toothy jaws clamped onto his throat, her hind-talons raking and tearing the silver disk that secured his wings. There was a sudden flash of light and a loud crackle and the dragon fell away, smoke pouring from her nostrils, as the silver disk peeled from Stonewall's back, spraying a shower of bright sparks.

Stonewall dropped, limp and seemingly lifeless, blood spurting from the wound to his neck. Anza spun once more, searching among the converging valkyries for one not attacking, and finally spotted the one peeling away from the action. This would be the gunpowder carrier. With all her strength, she hurled her tomahawk, aiming at the dragon's chest. Without waiting to see if the blow connected she dove, moving so fast the wind tore her leather vest at the seams. Arms outstretched, she shot toward Stonewall, catching him mere inches above the canopy. Before she could decide what to do next, a spear flashed past her right wing, missing by less than a yard. She glanced back to find that the dragon who carried the stolen powder sack was unharmed. The tomahawk tumbled uselessly as it fell, apparently having struck one of the armored plates covering her breast.

Everywhere Anza looked, dragons converged upon her. Stonewall was still breathing, but he was bleeding fast from his neck, blood pulsing out with each heartbeat. With a thought, she dropped toward the trees below, folding in her wings at the last second as she crashed through the canopy of leaves. She wrapped her thighs around Stonewall's torso as she grabbed at tree limbs, snapping them, but not before she swung him toward the fork of a large branch. As he landed, she opened her wings once more and dropped to his level. She grabbed him by the neck and pressed his wound shut with as much pressure as she could manage without crushing his windpipe.

She scanned the leaves above her. She heard the flapping of large wings coming closer, passing overhead, then veering off. Sky-dragons couldn't fly beneath the trees, and it wasn't their mission to kill her. They cared only about returning to the Nest with the stolen gunpowder.

Her only mission was to stop that. But if she removed her hand from Stonewall's neck, he'd be dead within minutes. She knew what her father would tell her to do. She knew the stakes of letting the valkyries get away. But her hand would not move. She waited, wondering when it would be time to let him go. The part of her that had always done everything her father asked of her without complaint or hesitation began to fret, worried about the distance the valkyries gained with each second. She was a cog in her father's machinery of war, and the gears of circumstance that pushed against her told her to fly, to fight, to obey her father and save mankind from the grim fate of dragons armed with gunpowder.

But something else, not a voice, not even truly a thought, told her that saving this one man was more important than saving her world.

She waited in the dark forest for hours, knowing that by now the dragons were long escaped, the gunpowder vanished into the impenetrable vaults beneath the Nest. Stonewall was still alive, though he showed no signs of waking. His pulse was weak and irregular. He shuddered with each breath, but she felt certain that the worst of the bleeding had stopped. She peeled her hand away, slowly, carefully, for her skin was glued to his by blood. She studied him closely as her hand came free. No fresh blood appeared. She cut a strip from his pants leg to wrap around his wounds to keep them from reopening, then, with a great deal of effort utterly lacking in grace, she pulled him from the fork of the tree and hugged him tightly to her, rising slowly, pushing through limbs and leaves, until she found herself in a brightening sky. The forest all around was full of birdsong as every living thing around her stirred to greet the dawn.

She flew slowly, barely faster than she could run, to avoid buffeting him with winds. It took over an hour to reach Dragon Forge. She could hear men shouting as she approached. She coughed as she descended through layers of smoke, landing in front of the ramshackle building off the main square that had been converted into a hospital.

A hundred men, maybe more, ran toward her. She heard her name shouted, along with cries of, "Stonewall! It's Stonewall!"

She was in a daze as someone took Stonewall from her arms to lay him on the ground. A half dozen men were needed to place him on a blanket and carry him into the hospital. She thought, perhaps, she'd said, "Thank you," to one of the men, but couldn't remember. Her thoughts seemed to vanish as quickly as they formed.

She felt feverish, the world a dream. The foundry smoke painted the world around her in shades of red as the morning sun sifted through the plumes. She felt as if she was floating, and realized, slowly, that she was. She'd never closed her wings. She should do that. She should fall, and let men come and carry her, to take her into the hospital, to save her leg, if it could be saved.

But she didn't fall. She was waiting. Again, her action was thoughtless, free of conscious intention or will. She knew only that she was waiting. And, at last, she understood who she was waiting for.

The crowd around her parted as a deep voice shouted, "Out of my way, damn you. Get out of my way! Let me through!"

As the last man stepped aside, she saw him, her father, limping toward her. She could hear the gears and springs in his false leg click and twang as he moved forward in haste. He wore the same clothes he'd worn when she'd departed on her mission. He looked haggard and drawn, no doubt having been awake all night. At the thought, an involuntary smile played at the edges of her mouth. Of course he'd been worried for her. She was, after all, his finest machine, and her loss would hurt him dearly.

"What happened?" he demanded as he reached her.

"Thorny's dead," she said, softly.

Burke's face went slack. "Did the dragons find out the truth about him?"

"He detonated a grenade. He killed himself, killed several dragons, and saved my life. The dragons know the truth about him."

"People are saying Stonewall's hurt. What happened? What went wrong?"

"I'm hurt," she said.

Burke's brow furrowed. "Your leg. How bad—"

"More than my leg," she said. "I think... something inside me... has broken. My... my gears have stopped turning. I couldn't finish the mission."

"You couldn't... the guns are still missing?"

"I believe the guns are destroyed. But valkyries escaped with gunpowder and a grenade. We gave chase and caught them and Stonewall nearly died. He... he would have bled out if I'd abandoned him. So I... I saved him. I let the valkyries escape."

"You what?" said Burke, his face turning red. "Don't you understand what you've done? The importance of this mission? Everything depended on you!"

"I know," said Anza.

"But faced with a choice between saving Stonewall or finishing the mission, you chose to save him?" asked Burke, running a hand through his hair, no longer looking straight at her.

"It wasn't truly a choice," said Anza. "I did what I did. I can't explain why."

Burke nodded. "I can. I know exactly why."

She stared at him numbly, waiting for his rebuke.

Instead, he stepped forward and closed his arms around her. With his lips next to her ear, he whispered, his voice nearly a sob, "I'm so sorry, so, so sorry. You've got a good heart, Anza. A better heart than I ever had. I wish so much the world was different. I want so much to never send you into danger again."

"But you will," she whispered back.

"I will," he answered. "Not because I want to. But because I want to make a world where no father need ever wait up all night wondering what the dragons have done to his child. I'm sorry. I'm sorry."

"I will always be your song of death," she murmured, her voice dreamy and distant.

"No," he said, his voice choking. "You'll always be my daughter."

Then her wings folded musically and she collapsed into her father's arms, overcome by exhaustion, and overwhelmed by the realization that, in truth, he loved her.

The adventure continues in DRAGONSGATE.

A BITTERWOOD BESTIARY

DRAGON RACES

SUN-DRAGONS

Sun-dragons are the lords of the realm, possessing forty-foot wingspans and long, toothy jaws that can bite a man in half. Sun-dragons are adorned with crimson scales tipped with highlights of orange and yellow that give them a fiery appearance. Wispy feathers around their snouts give the illusion that they breathe smoke. Though gifted with natural weaponry and a tough, scaly hide, sun-dragons are intelligent tool-users who recognize the value of using spears and armor to enhance their already formidable combat skills. Politically, sun-dragons are traditionally organized under an all-powerful king, who, by rights, owns all property within the kingdom. A close network of other sun-dragons, often related to the king, manage individual abodes within the kingdom. The current "king" is Hex, the only surviving son of the old king Albekizan. Hex is a political radical with anarchist leanings, and as a result of his refusal to perform the duties of a king, the sun-dragon political structures are currently in great disarray.

SKY-DRAGONS

Half the size of sun-dragons, sky-dragons are a race devoted to scholarship. Most male sky-dragons dwell at colleges built around large libraries. Their leaders are known as biologians, a position that is part priest, part librarian, and part scientist. Most male sky-dragons distain combat, but a few are selected to either serve in the king's elite aerial guard, or if they show a talent for brutality, become part of the ranks of slave-catchers than keep human slaves compliant. Sky-dragons practice strict segregation of the sexes. The females of the species dwell on an island fortress known as the Nest, defended by fierce warriors known as valkyries. The scholars among the females tend to focus on more practical disciplines than their male counterparts, and are particularly well known for their talents as engineers.

EARTH-DRAGONS

Wingless creatures, earth-dragons are humanoids with turtle-beaked faces and broad, muscular bodies. They are much stronger than men, but also much slower. As a race, they have few valuable skills beyond their enthusiasm for hitting things. This makes them excellent soldiers and decent blacksmiths. Except for the rare periods of time when earth-dragons are in heat, it's nearly impossible to tell the difference between the two sexes of earth-dragon. They are the only dragon species to lay eggs instead of producing live birth. Very rarely, some earth-dragons are born with a chameleon mutation that allows them to blend into their surroundings. These mutant dragons are also smarter and faster than their brethren and are usually recruited to become assassins for the dragon king, serving in a greatly feared unit known as the Black Silence.

LESSER SPECIES

HUMANS

Humans live in the margins of dragon society as slaves, pets, and prey. The sun-dragons tolerate their existence primarily because of mankind's natural talent for farming; the labor of humans keeps the bellies of dragons full. Humans are generally peaceful and harmless in small, isolated groups, but quick to war with other tribes. Recently, a prophet named Ragnar united many of the men in the kingdom into a rebel army. The rebellion successfully seized the town of Dragon Forge, and a man named Burke is using the town's foundries to create new weapons that may forever alter the balance of power between man and dragon... assuming the humans can resist their natural urges to go to war with themselves.

LONG-WYRMS

Fifty-foot long copper colored serpents with fourteen pairs of legs, long-wyrms are ferocious carnivores, and, fortunately, exceedingly rare.

GREAT-LIZARDS

Often used as beasts of burden, great-lizards are twenty food long reptiles that closely resemble giant iguanas with a more upright stance.

OX-DOGS

The product of centuries of careful breeding, ox-dogs are the largest canine species ever to exist, standing nearly six feet high at the shoulder. Despite their fearsome build, most are docile in temperament, though earth-dragons often train them for hunting and have taught some to have an appetite for human flesh.

ABOUT THE AUTHOR

James Maxey's mother warned him if he read too many comic books they'd warp his mind. She was right. Now an adult who can't stop daydreaming, James is unsuited for decent work and ekes out a pittance writing down demented fantasies about masked women, fiery dragons, and monkeys.

Traditionally, this is where we list all the books he's written but at this point it's a pretty long list, and honestly, I don't feel like typing them all out. He's also won some award and honors, like being named Piedmont Laureate. If you really want to know, just google him.

James lives in Hillsborough, North Carolina with his lovely and patient wife Cheryl and too many cats. For additional information about James and his writing, visit jamesmaxey.net. There's probably something on there about signing up for his newsletter and getting free stuff, like pizza. Well, probably not pizza. Short stories maybe? I bet he gives away free short stories. Writers are kind of cheap.

Proof

26411128R00098

Made in the USA
Columbia, SC
10 September 2018